FLOWERS FOR
RODNEY

Dave, Sherry, Hunter and Brooke,
Find strength in each
other and the power of your
beautiful family!

Kristine E. Brickey

ISBN: 1492343285
ISBN 13: 9781492343288
Library of Congress Control Number: 2014901096
CreateSpace Independent Publishing Platform
North Charleston, South Carolina

Find strength in each
other and the power of your
Beautiful Family!
Kristine Brickey

Rodney Birge leaned back and guzzled the can of cheap beer without stopping for air. His cohort in crime, Alan, laughed as he puffed on the joint they'd been sharing in the front seat of Rodney's beat up white El Camino parked in the back of the school lot in Oxford, Connecticut.

"Beats sitting in class, right?" Rodney smirked, shaking shaggy dark brown bangs over his equally dark eyes. Alan pounded the dashboard as he coughed and laughed in agreement.

"Mel's going to be pissed when she finds out we didn't grab her on our way out here!" Alan added, a flash of fear in his eyes betraying his attempt to be lighthearted.

Melinda Jo Hawkins was Rodney's angry counterpart of their group, the crew. Tossed around from one foster home to another since she was young, Mel made no attempt to be civil with most people. Her unnaturally black hair, facial piercings, and always too heavy black eyeliner were a reflection of her inner self. Melinda was willing to fight before asking questions and had battle scars to prove her toughness.

Sitting in the car now with Alan, Rodney remembered his first up close and personal with Melinda. He rather drunkenly crashed next to her on a couch one night during a party. Melinda looked at him with daggers but then stayed where she was, her shoulder pressed into Rodney's as his weight pulled her toward him. With exaggerated slowness, Rodney reached over and wrapped a hand around the bright purple streak of hair tucked behind Melinda's ear. Instead of attacking, Melinda allowed the touch. They both laughed, shared a joint, and that was it.

Rodney was prime for the picking, angry about too many things, and busy hating his mom. Before long he, Mel, Alan and a few tagalongs were the crew. Alan seemed to appreciate Rodney's ability to temper Mel's outbursts, as Alan was often the person Mel went after when she was out of control.

"She's not even here today," Rodney said, laughing as Alan's blue eyes closed in relief.

Through the smoky haze and bloodshot eyes, Rodney watched as the overweight and underpaid school security cop came out of the building. Rodney could have started the car. He had plenty of time to flee the scene. Something inside of him made him just sit and watch. He felt too tired to ask his slender muscled frame to move. *Let it come,* he thought. His mom wouldn't be surprised and she might even be glad to be rid of him. Getting busted would break his probation, but nothing was getting easier anyway.

"Hey, Alan, look at Bozo coming our way," Rodney warned.

It seemed like he was watching a slow motion movie as Alan cursed, shoved his contraband into the glove box, and opened his car door to dash away into the lot and away from Rodney.

"Here we go again, Ma," Rodney whispered as he rolled down the driver's window and waited for whatever might happen next.

• • •

Susan leaned against the counter focusing on the arrangement of roses and baby's breath, certain that it was an apology bouquet. Based on the extravagance, it had been quite an *oops* on someone's part. She couldn't help but wonder if the woman would forgive or take the flowers and vanish. Sighing, Susan pulled her long brown hair into a ponytail, the shop lights glinting off the sun kissed highlights of blondes and reds.

Wrapping the dozens of flowers in cellophane held together with red satin ribbon, she heard the soft jingle of bells from the front door. Looking up and walking toward the register, she was already smiling at the customer.

"Ah, that'll do the trick," he said, pulling his wallet from his pocket.

"Big trouble, huh?" Susan chuckled as she ran his card through the machine. The man grinned in agreement as he signed the slip.

Handing him the arrangement, she wished him a good night. After he'd gone, she locked the door, flipping the open sign to read closed. Pulling down the shade, she took a deep breath and enjoyed her shop, her dream come true after years of hard work and longing. It was hard to believe that she was an independent businesswoman. More than just a way of financial survival, her flowers let her escape everyday life, hiding for a time from the drama caused by the son she'd tried to protect and who now seemed eager to ruin his life.

The ringing of her cell phone broke her daydream, and Susan dragged her phone out of her deep apron pocket. Oxford City Police Department glared at her from the caller ID screen. For one horrible moment, she thought about not answering. She knew it was Rodney, again in some sort of trouble that was never his fault. There was always a story to lay blame at someone else's feet. The teachers had it out for him. The principal didn't like the way he dressed. The police were stupid pigs who stopped him for no reason. She had heard all the excuses over the last two years or so of escalating problems.

"Susan Birge here," she said quietly into the phone, standing as tall and strong as her five and a half foot frame allowed.

"Ma'am, this is Sergeant Bullion, from OCPD. We have your son here, and we're going to need you to come down and collect him."

"I'll be right there," she said. Susan closed her brown eyes, fighting the tears that were welling up.

"We're located at—"

Susan interrupted. "Thank you, officer. I am familiar with where your station is located."

• • •

When Susan went into the two-story brick building, she was surprised by the calmness. Entering the reception area, she had to pass through security, letting the officer search her purse and run the wand over her. Finding nothing, Susan was allowed into the desk area, and she asked about Rodney's case.

As she waited for the arresting officer, Susan forced herself to think about Rodney's newest delinquent behaviors and possible punishment. He had been such a sweet baby, and there were times even now that Susan could look past the anger that was almost constantly on his face and see the cherub she used to play patty-cake with, spending hours blowing kisses on his round, little belly. Closing her eyes for a brief moment, she allowed herself a smile of remembrance.

Suddenly, she was assaulted with the angry voice of her son coming from farther down the hallway. Fighting back tears, Susan turned her head to see Rodney in handcuffs being none too gently led through a gated door into the holding cell area of the station. Rodney saw her out of the corner of his eye. He turned to continue screaming at the officer standing in the hall and then began yelling at Susan.

"Get me outta here, Ma! They don't have anything on me. It was all a setup and none of that stuff is mine! Get me out Ma, or I swear!"

Susan saw the rage and hatred on his face, harshness so clear that the earlier vision of his baby face was blindly erased from her mind. The door latched loudly behind Rodney and the escorting officer. Susan dropped her head and let the tears fall.

She swiped her eyes on the sleeve of her coat as an officer approached her from where Rodney had disappeared. Susan stood, noticing that he was quite tall and though stern his green eyes didn't appear to have the judgmental expression she expected. His broad build promised strength that would allow control of any confrontation, and Susan hoped Rodney hadn't tried his luck too harshly.

"Mrs. Birge?" he asked, extending his hand to shake Susan's in greeting. "I'm Officer Phillip Reynolds."

"Ms. Birge, but yes, that's me. What has he done now?" Susan asked, trying to keep the sob out of her voice.

"Why don't we go back to my desk, where I can fill you in while your son is being processed, ma'am?"

Susan followed him into the larger room behind the imposing reception desk, sitting in the chair that he motioned her toward. Declining the offered cup of coffee or soft drink, Susan sighed and awaited the bad news.

She listened as Officer Reynolds went through the list of Rodney's newest offenses. Apparently, Rodney had once again decided that skipping school was an option. However, rather than leave like he and his buddies usually did, they had opted to sit in the school parking lot and enjoy a relaxing joint while they discussed their plans for the rest of the day. Unfortunately for the two boys, the school security guard had noticed the smoke. When he realized it was not just a smoking-on-school-property violation he had called the local police for assistance. Noticing the guard Rodney's friend had made a quick exit, but Rodney had laughed and leaned back to finish his smoke.

Rodney had baited the guard, taunting him with mall-cop jokes while the guard moved around the car taking down the license plate information, stalling until the police arrived. With the bravado of drugs in his system, her son had opened up the cooler in the backseat, offering the guard a beer while they waited, thinking he was free and clear, laughing when the school officer casually reached over and accepted the can.

That was when the patrol car had pulled up, and Rodney's laughter turned quickly to rage as his high evaporated in sudden understanding. To make matters worse, a search of the car had turned up an unlicensed handgun in the glove box. Rodney had sworn it wasn't his, but he wasn't going to rat out his buddy who had left him to fend for himself either. As the owner of the vehicle, Rodney would be charged.

Susan listened quietly as Officer Reynolds listed the final charges of minor in possession of alcohol, minor in possession of marijuana and related drug paraphernalia, possession of a handgun, and of course the inevitable resisting arrest.

"Your boy put up quite a fight, Ms. Birge, and I'm sorry to say that it didn't stop even after he was in the patrol car. He was quite exuberant in his expletives for the entire ride to the department," the officer explained.

"Yes, well, I'm not surprised, Officer Reynolds," Susan said sadly. "At least I know I can count on Rodney in that area." She sighed and took advantage of the tissues on the desk, wiping her eyes before looking the policeman in the eyes. "So, what next then?" she asked.

"Well, I'm afraid that there will be certain consequences that are up to the school, since it occurred on their property. In addition, depending on Rodney's willingness to take responsibility and agree to make some changes, the degree of legal trouble he'll be in could also vary tremendously."

"When will he be able to come home?" Susan asked, guiltily admitting to herself that a few days of being able to go to work without worrying about Rodney seemed like a small piece of paradise at the moment.

"Once he's done with processing, you can make his bail and he can leave with you tonight," he explained.

"Tonight? He can leave tonight even with the drug and firearm charges?" Susan was appalled. "What about his current probation? This will violate his terms and put him back in front of Judge Garcia, won't it?" She sounded desperate even to her own ears. She simply couldn't believe that the system would allow there to be such leniency.

"Well, that will be up to the court to decide, Ms. Birge. Don't you want to take your son home tonight?" He was watching her closely now, and Susan was aware that she should perhaps be very careful as to how she answered this question.

"It's just that, well, at least if Rodney is here, I'll know where he is tonight. If I take him home, he's bound to try to meet up with his friend who fled so they can get their stories straight. He just doesn't listen to me anymore, and I seem to be waiting every time the phone rings to hear that he's done something even worse than the previous stunt..." Susan stopped herself as she felt the hysteria rising in her voice.

"I'm sorry, but I'm just, well, so very very tired of feeling out of control with my own child," Susan confessed. "Does it make me a horrid mother to want to leave him here tonight? To need one night of peace where I don't lay awake in bed listening to him trying to sneak out, or worse, sneak back into the house, thinking I don't know he's been gone?"

Officer Reynolds knew defeat when he saw it and the woman in front of him had all the classic signs. He had seen her son's criminal history, and it was long and detailed, filled with drug and alcohol abuse, violence, and a general disregard for any type of authority, parental or other.

"It makes you human, ma'am," he said quietly. Susan could see Officer Reynold's green eyes watching her and felt his mental wheels spinning as he evaluated her and the situation. She should feel bad, should feel worse than bad actually. All she could do now though was wait for him to decide, sensing that he would make the right decision based on what he saw in her eyes and had seen in the face of her belligerent, angry teenager.

"He'll need to go up in front of the judge tomorrow for arraignment, and since you feel Rodney would quickly violate the conditions of his being released on bond, it's probably best that he stay overnight here, Ms. Birge," Officer Reynolds said slowly, giving her both a night's peace and also offering an olive branch from the guilt he knew she'd be riddled with by leaving her son in jail overnight.

"He'll be safe here, Ms. Birge," Officer Reynolds continued. "We're a pretty small town, and he'll be kept in a holding cell alone. I'll also make sure he's put on a general watch, to be sure he doesn't try to hurt himself in any way." He could see her relief as Susan's shoulders relaxed, the immediate panic leaving her eyes.

"Thank you so much, Officer." Susan exhaled. "I cannot tell you how much this means to me."

"Just check in with the front desk before you leave, and the sergeant will be able to give you the information you'll need for your son's hearing tomorrow," he explained. He stood and led the frazzled mother back into the front of the department.

"Should I see Rodney before I go?" Susan asked suddenly. Officer Reynolds could feel tension leaping off her body at the idea of having to face the anger that was sure to be there when Rodney figured out that he would not be going home tonight.

"I'm afraid that won't be allowed, Ms. Birge," he said. "Rodney will be in booking for quite a while, and then he'll need to go into the holding cell until he sobers up."

"Of course, well then, thank you," Susan said as she swung open the door into the dark autumn night. The glass door shut behind her, leaving Officer Reynolds looking at his own image as he stood in the brightly lit building watching Susan Birge walk away.

She felt beaten and exhausted. *Oh, Rodney, what have you gotten yourself into this time?* Susan worried as she drove to her empty home. Knowing Rodney was sobering up in a cell for now but possibly headed into much worse trouble spun her thoughts into knots. There would be no easy sleep tonight.

2

Rodney found himself alone in the cell, but at least the cuffs had been removed once he'd stopped fighting the officers and cussing them up and down. He was furious with his mother and almost as mad at the officer who had come in to tell Rodney that his mother was not going to be posting his bond and taking him home. Reynolds had probably been yucking it up the whole time, laughing with his pig cop buddies about how Rodney's own mother knew he was such a loser.

Thinking about it made Rodney want to punch something hard enough to break his own bones and mash out the pain that rushed through his head. That good for nothing bitch had left him here to rot, and he began to imagine all of the ways he could get revenge for this betrayal.

Of course, it wasn't the first time his mother had betrayed him. She thought she was so perfect, but Rodney knew that wasn't true. If she had been, his father would have stayed around and been there to raise him.

Sitting in the holding cell gave him plenty of time to review his life and Rodney could feel the seething rage begin to build anew. Rodney was only two when his mother had thrown his dad out to fend for himself. He didn't remember his dad very much, of course, since he had been so little, but his sister, Taylor, had told him all about what had happened. Of course, Taylor had totally taken their mom's side, and stuck up for her throwing their dad out like the weekly garbage.

Taylor was eight years older than Rodney, so her memories were much stronger than his could be about their father. Once he'd been old enough to begin asking questions, Rodney had tried to get his mom to explain. He still vividly remembered coming home from first grade, dried tears on his face. A local Boy Scout group came to his school, passing out information about joining, telling the boys how much fun it would be to spend quality time doing things with their dads. There would be camping and hiking and learning to tie cool knots and even weekend trips.

As Rodney reached out his hand to take the pamphlet, the little boy next to him said to the Boy Scout representative, "Rodney doesn't have a dad." Rodney's fantasy bubble of outdoorsy father-and-son days burst and so did his temper.

Standing up quickly, he shouted, "I do to have a dad! He's the best dad ever!" Then Rodney shoved the other boy with both hands, completely knocking the chair backward and over, before running into the hallway and out onto the sidewalk leaving the school behind him. He rushed home to find his mother and try to learn the truth about why his dad wasn't around like all the other kids' dads were for them.

When Rodney finally made his way the short distance to his mother's house, the little sidewalk path leading up to the front door suddenly seemed an endless distance. He looked up, knowing that he was going to start crying again, and saw his mother standing on the front porch. She didn't say anything, just knelt down and opened her arms as he bolted into the safety of her embrace. For a long time, Rodney simply let himself stand in her hug, feeling her heartbeat, smelling her familiar vanilla perfume, and taking deep breaths until he felt better.

"What happened, baby?" she finally asked, as she stood and led him inside. Rodney told her that the kids at school had been mean. As his mom asked more questions, Rodney saw the strain come into her face. Even at six, he could see how she changed. He was too young to know it was feelings of guilt and sadness that overwhelmed her. She tried to tell him that their family was special, and that even though his dad was gone she loved Rodney enough for two parents.

She even offered to let Rodney join the Scouts with her as the adult. Obviously the school had called, so she knew all about what had really happened that day. Rodney told her he never wanted to go back to that stupid place, but of course that didn't work out for him either. The teacher had talked to the class and explained that Rodney had been very upset, but that he was sorry about what had happened. When he returned to school the next day the other little boy apologized to Rodney about what he had said and Rodney apologized for pushing and yelling. The teacher smiled, thinking she had full control of the situation.

However, from that day on, there were occasional skirmishes between Rodney and the other kids as the name calling and taunting continued and Rodney's burning resentment was fueled by his loss and confusion.

The clanging of a cell door somewhere down the hallway brought Rodney back to the hard bench he was sitting on, the sterile room where he would be spending the night before heading into court tomorrow. The names he'd been called seemed as fresh as the days they'd happened. Closing his eyes, it was easy for Rodney to slip back into his memories.

Rodney was eleven, suspended from school and grounded from everything that made his life worth living until he got his act together. He heard Taylor come home, calling out for him but he was ignoring her. Taylor had been bugging him for the last week about being nice to their mom. She was leaving for college soon, and was on his case about everything lately. Her nagging was what had set him off and ended up in his getting suspended for fighting again.

He heard his bedroom door open, and felt his older sister flop down on top of his quilt. Rodney sighed in disgust, throwing his best bug off look at Taylor, but she just laughed and tousled his hair.

"Mom told me what happened, buddy," Taylor said. Rodney was surprised when tears filled Taylor's eyes. "I'm sorry this is so hard for you, but you have to believe me that Mom did the right thing when she saved us from our dad."

Rodney couldn't know that Taylor remembered the yelling and fighting that had gone on for years, leaving their mother with bruised arms and days on end when she refused to take off the big sunglasses that Taylor thought at first were super cool. Once she figured out the dark glasses were to cover the black eyes, Taylor hadn't thought they were so cool.

"Listen," she began. "I know you're all angry, but there are things you don't remember. There are reasons we left, Rodney," Taylor tried.

Without giving him a chance, Taylor finally shared the big story, trying to get Rodney to understand why he had no father.

Their mother had decided on leaving their dad, she explained to her little brother. Taylor had gone to bed, anxious for the next day to get there so she and her mom could go away together and live somewhere not so scary all of the time. Her mother had told her that she was telling dad that night, and that if he would get help and could get better then maybe they could come back one day.

Sometime later that night, Taylor woke up to a crashing sound and then sudden silence. She was seven years old and terrified to open her bedroom door. She called out for her mom as loudly as she could, but her mother didn't respond. Taylor knew then that something was very wrong.

Trembling with fear at what she might or might not find, Taylor crept to her doorway and cracked open the door. Whispering for her mother, Taylor looked into a scene of destruction. The beautiful vase of flowers that her mother had spent so much time arranging on the family room table was smashed on the floor along with the lamp. Taylor's own big-girl bookshelf was tipped over, and she could see her storybooks strewn across the floor. Rushing into the room, Taylor had reached for her favorite book and that was when she heard the whimper.

Turning her head toward the sound, Taylor saw her mother lying on her bedroom floor as her father knelt beside her muttering. A small animal noise escaped Taylor. Her father looked at her and started to cry.

"Dad, what did you do?" Taylor screamed as she rushed over to her mother.

"Mom, wake up!" she yelled over and over. After a few minutes, Taylor looked up into the face of her father and began yelling at him to call the ambulance. Her father seemed incapable of moving and Taylor finally got up and made the 9-1-1 call herself.

An ambulance arrived shortly afterward, along with the police, who took her father away in handcuffs. Taylor spent that night with the neighbor, old Mrs. Arlen, until her mother came home the next day, her arm in a sling, walking very stiffly. Mrs. Arlen tried to talk to Susan, but Taylor saw her mother bow her head, cupping her hand over her belly as if in explanation.

The next day her father came home full of apologies with a small bouquet of flowers. As he broke down and cried, laying his head in her lap, their mom sat motionless at the kitchen table.

"Never again, Joe," her mother said. "There's another baby joining this family and the violence has to end. Now. Things have to change."

Susan looked over at her daughter, and Taylor said she'd never forget the defeated look in their mother's eyes as she sat with tears running down her face, placing her hand in resignation on her sobbing husband's shoulder. Taylor told Rodney that their father had promised that he would never hurt any of them again, repeating how much he loved them and saying how sorry he was for everything.

Sitting now in the cell, Rodney wasn't sure how much of Taylor's stories could even be believed. His mother had never seemed afraid of anything that he could remember. No matter what had happened, his mother was there to battle for him and Taylor. She had never said a bad word to him about his father, always telling Rodney when he asked that his father had loved him very much. How could his mother, so independent and strong-willed be the same person that allowed the things that Taylor described?

So, when Rodney found himself at a loss, filled with the anger that overcame him at times, he struck out at Susan with all his pent-up fury. He blamed his mother for not bailing him out and vowed that when she showed up for his hearing in the morning, if she showed up for his hearing, that he would ignore her and make her fully understand how pissed he was for this latest betrayal; because betrayal was exactly how Rodney saw it as he stewed in his cell.

When a small bit of conscience tugged at him, reminding him of all the times his mom had tried to help him, Rodney pushed it away. When the guilt of past actions tried to race through his mind, all of the problems at school and his run-ins with the law, he shrugged it off as nothing. Rodney clung to his mother's latest betrayal, ignoring all of the goodness and the memories of what his sister had tried to tell him. He fell asleep on a pillow of righteous indignation, unaware and uncaring of his mother's pain.

3

Susan approached the courthouse the next afternoon filled with dread. She was fully aware of how Rodney would treat her when he saw her in court. However, armed with a full night's sleep she felt stronger than she had in months. Knowing that somewhere deep inside her teenager was goodness and strength, she was willing to do whatever it might take to help her struggling son.

As she entered the hallway leading to Courtroom C, Susan saw Officer Reynolds seated on a nearby bench. He stood and smiled at her, and she couldn't help noticing how handsome he was up close.

"Good morning, Ms. Birge," he said. "You look rested."

Susan smiled back, nodding in agreement. "It's amazing what a good night of sleep can do for the body and soul," she said.

Phillip couldn't help but notice how good Susan looked standing in front of him in a simple yet very striking dark-brown suit. The green and gold in her shirt put a sparkle in her eyes that hadn't been there the night before; or at least if it had been, the sadness of the situation had kept it hidden.

"Well, I guess I should be getting in, just in case Rodney's already inside," Susan explained. She went to open the imposing door. Before she could reach it herself, Phillip stretched out his arm and opened the door for her, indicating with a slight nod of his head that she should go in before him.

"Thank you, Officer Reynolds," Susan said.

"My mother would have my head if I neglected to hold the door for a lady," he said with a chuckle as Susan entered the courtroom.

With a smile on her face, Susan turned into the room and walked directly into the angry glare of her son Rodney. He shook his head in disgust when he noticed who Susan had been talking to. He turned away and pointedly ignored Susan, looking out into the space of the room.

Susan sighed and went to sit up near the front where she knew that even as Rodney tried to play the tough guy and ignore her, he would still be able to see her there in his support.

There were a number of cases on the docket before Rodney's was called, but finally his was up. Susan waited patiently as the numerous charges were read and the public defender assigned to Rodney's case stated that his client would be pleading not guilty. In addition, the lawyer assured the court that Rodney could safely remain in the care and custody of his mother until the trial.

The judge flipped slowly through the large file before him, glancing up occasionally at Rodney as he read a passage here and there. Rodney sat slumped in the hard-backed chair until the public defender leaned over and quietly said something at which point Rodney sat up a bit. Susan wished desperately that her son would at least stop glaring long enough to appear somewhat remorseful or abashed at his actions. Rodney's personal defense had always been the standard, "It's someone else's fault," so he probably didn't think he needed to feel ashamed of anything once again.

"Young man," the judge said suddenly. "Are you aware of how many opportunities you have had to change your ways?"

"Your Honor," the lawyer started, "if it pleases the court," but that was as far as he got before the judge interrupted him with a look that made it clear there would be no more interruptions.

"Son, you have been here too many times. I see your mother sitting behind you, and I wonder if you have any empathy at all

for how your behavior affects her. You are currently on probation for your previous violations of the law, and yet you continue
to behave in a reckless and belligerent manner."

The judge leaned deeply into his red, high-backed, leather
chair and looked over to where Officer Reynolds was seated
with the prosecutor. These cases brought the judge nothing but
heartache, especially when he could see a glimmer of something
good in the defendant. He'd been a defiant, angry young man
himself for a number of years before a concerned truancy officer
had gotten hold of him and straightened his sorry behind out,
setting him on a positive track.

Looking down at the latest addition to Rodney Birge's file to
check the arresting officer's name, the judge sighed and straightened up to his full seated height.

"Officer Reynolds, as the arresting officer I am asking
whether or not you think the young man seated before me
deserves another chance. In your opinion, can he or can he not
be trusted to behave while out on bond?"

Phillip sat for a moment contemplating the question, looking over at Rodney who still stared straight ahead, glaring at a
spot somewhere deep in the floor before him. In his peripheral
vision Phillip could see Susan sitting up straight, her hands tightly
clenched in her lap. There was a part of Phillip that wanted to
end the turmoil for this woman, and tell the judge that this bad
seed should be given the severest punishment allowable. He
knew that would not give Susan peace, and neither would it help
her reach whatever good that still remained.

"Honestly, your Honor, letting Rodney Birge off the hook
for these latest crimes will not be in his best interest," Officer
Reynolds began as his answer. He could see Susan's face tighten
as his words hit her, and even Rodney's stare broke momentarily
before he wrapped himself back in a protective shell.

"However, we both know that once a juvenile believes himself
to be above the law there isn't much to prevent his getting into
more serious trouble very quickly."

"I completely agree with you, Officer Reynolds," said the judge. "Which is why I will be remanding custody of Rodney Birge to his mother on a conditional bond if Rodney wishes to stay out of a juvenile detention facility."

Susan could feel her body tremble. Rodney was not going to jail, at least not right now. She was instantly relieved and then just as suddenly horrified by the prospect of having him at home to get into even more trouble.

"Stand up, young man," the judge directed sternly to Rodney. Rodney and his attorney both stood to face the judge's directive.

"First of all, you will be at school every day, and each and every hour of the day. If you fail to show up, I will have you picked up for failure to comply with a court order. Is that understood?"

Rodney's defender answered quickly, "Yes, of course, Your Honor."

"Not from you, Mr. Smith. I'd like to hear directly from your client that he is willing and able to comply with the stipulations that go along with his bond."

Rodney nodded his head glumly and when the judge glared and raised an eyebrow, Rodney straightened up and answered with a loud and clear, "Yes…Your Honor."

"That's better, young man. Now, the second stipulation is that you will be required to fulfill a number of community service hours. Directly after school each day you will walk from the front of your school to the Oxford Youth Center where you will do whatever you are told to do by the Director of Services there, a Mr. Thomas Rodriguez. Is this clear?"

"Yes, Your Honor, but wouldn't it be okay if I drove to the center?" Rodney answered but this time with slightly more attitude in his voice. Susan could see him letting anger at what he felt an unjust punishment get under his skin. She only hoped he'd be able to hold it together long enough to not blow up at the judge before she could get him out of here.

"And what is it you believe you would be driving, Mr. Birge?" the judge asked Rodney. "Your car has been impounded and claimed as evidence in a drug-related crime. In addition, because of your repeat offender status, your driver's license has been revoked until further notice. Until you prove to this court that you can be trusted, you will not be allowed to drive or to be unsupervised for that matter."

Rodney was stunned. He hadn't even considered the possibility that the court could take his ride.

"Furthermore," added the judge, "you will be required to fulfill weekly, random drug and alcohol testing, so I strongly suggest that you stay away from poor influences. There will be a no-tolerance stand on further abuses."

Waves of animosity rolled off Rodney, and Susan could see his fists clench into whiteness against the top of the table. *Here it comes,* she thought, silently urging Rodney to keep his temper in check.

"Is there a problem, young man?" asked the judge very calmly as he leaned back once again in the imposing leather throne.

"No, sir, it's just that puts quite an imposition on my mother, what with her trying to run her own business and babysit me too," Rodney added.

"Yes, it is quite an imposition, Rodney, which is something you should have thought about before you created this latest problem for everyone involved."

He was good. Susan had to give the judge credit. Of course, he had probably been dealing with kids like Rodney for years.

"Since you mentioned it though, Mr. Birge, perhaps we should ask your mother if she is willing to undertake this, as you called it, imposition on her time and energy. She may simply prefer to send you to a facility such as the juvenile detention camps we have located in this fine state of Connecticut."

Susan found herself suddenly under the attention of all eyes in the courtroom. If her nerves had been shot before, it was nothing compared to what she felt now. For a brief moment, the juvenile detention camp swam before her eyes as a way out. Was it time to give up? Had she simply done all she could to help

Rodney? Could she even remember a time when Rodney had given her anything but trouble and anxious days and nights?

"Please stand, Ms. Birge," the judge said to her.

As she rose, Susan looked up at the judge. She held her head high, shoulders back, and chin up as she refused to look away from the silent challenge in the judge's face.

"So, what say you to this imposition your son's actions have placed upon you today in this courtroom? Are you willing to be his babysitter as he put it? Are you able to take on this burden?"

Susan moved her eyes to look straight at Rodney. His brown eyes so like his father's looked back into her green gaze. She remembered how when he was little he would come up to her, squeezing her face gently between his chubby, dimpled hands, and tell her in his sweet baby voice that he loved her up to the moon and over the sun. It had been their special saying, and it had been so long since he'd said it to her. Despite the years of problems, he was still her baby boy, and she knew there was nothing she wouldn't do to try and save him even if it was from himself.

Smiling quietly at Rodney, Susan looked back at the judge. "My son is never a burden to me, Your Honor. His actions and behaviors, yes; but Rodney is my child, my responsibility, and my life. Of course I will help him follow the rules that you have laid out for him. I want nothing more than for my son to get his life back on a positive track and to build a future for himself that he can be proud of."

"Well, Mr. Birge, it looks like we have a deal then. I warn you, however, if you fail to follow my directives, Officer Reynolds here will be picking you up and delivering you personally to the Connecticut Juvenile Offenders' Detention and Rehabilitation Center. At this point, Officer Reynolds will simply be checking in to insure that you stay the course, so to speak. You're going to need all the help you can get young man in order to stay away from the poor influences of the friends you have, the drugs and alcohol, and to get back on the path you need to find your way to a bright future."

Rodney stood still, waiting out what might come next. Susan was watching him, and a shiver of apprehension ran down her spine. Rodney was far too calm after hearing the judge's stipulations, and she could almost see the hamster spinning its wheel in his brain. She feared Rodney was already figuring out ways to bypass the system, as he'd been able to do so often in the past.

The judge wasn't quite finished, however, and Susan had an eerie feeling that he had read her mind, or at the very least been able to foresee Rodney's at work. "In addition, Rodney, to assist your mother in her monitoring and to help you avoid any further temptations, you will also be equipped with an electronic ankle tether."

Susan could see Rodney clench once again, but knew that as angry as her son must be, he also wasn't a complete dolt. Rodney wouldn't give up this easily, yet he knew when to cede and await a battle more likely of going in his favor.

As the palpable tension filled the court, Rodney's defense attorney finally stood and thanked the judge for his generous deal, eyeing Rodney from the corner of his eye while doing so, just in case his client snapped.

"Therefore, I wish you strength, Rodney. Ms. Birge, once the necessary paperwork is filled out, you are free to take your son home. This case is now closed until a satisfactory length of time has passed wherein the defendant must prove himself worthy of this additional chance to change his life around. Trial is set for six months."

The banging of the gavel was the last straw for Susan's nerves. She sat down suddenly on the wooden bench and watched Rodney be escorted out of the courtroom to the out processing area without even turning back to glance at her. Funny, how a few minutes ago she had felt so strong facing the judge and these newest responsibilities. Now, she thought fleetingly of running back to the judge's chambers and begging him to change his mind and place Rodney anywhere but with her.

She looked up as she felt a presence beside her and saw Officer Reynolds watching her. "Change of heart?" he asked, smiling.

"Is it that obvious?" Susan asked, her voice quivering.

"No one would blame you if you did," he told her.

"Yes, yes *he* would, Officer Reynolds," she said looking at the closed door where Rodney had exited.

"Since we'll probably be seeing a bit of each other, please call me Phillip. Phillip Reynolds, your son's new conscience," he said smiling.

"Fine, but then no more ma'am or Ms. Birge. I'm just Susan," she said, standing and reaching out to shake his hand, noticing the strength of his grip and the warmth of his fingers around her own.

"Deal," he said. "Now, do you know where to go and collect Rodney?" he asked, already concerned that Susan seemed nervous about the prospect of gaining custody of her troubled and self-destructive teenager.

"Yes, been here and done that, remember?" She tried to laugh but didn't quite manage it.

As Phillip walked her out into the hallway, Susan turned in the direction she needed to head, smiling and shaking her head.

"What is it?" he asked.

"So much has happened in the last twenty-four hours," Susan said. "I feel like this is a new start for Rodney, but I also have a horrible feeling that this is his last chance. Like, it's now or never; and I've never felt like this before. I'm relieved and terrified all at the same time."

"Susan, if you don't mind me saying so," Phillip answered, "from the short time I've seen you in action, I think the judge knew exactly how strong of a person he was putting in charge of Rodney. You seem to have done pretty well so far."

Susan looked up at him for a moment, taking a deep breath to clear her doubts. "Right, so onward to the next lap in the race, huh?"

Phillip smiled back as Susan straightened her shoulders, gently shook her loose hair, and walked down the hallway to gather her son from the system once again. He wasn't sure what was going to happen, but if he were a betting man, he'd lay odds on Susan Birge to win more rounds than she lost.

4

"**A**re you all right, son?" his mother asked him as Rodney sulked against the passenger seat of the car. He could not believe that he'd been forced to forfeit his car and now would have to be chauffeured around in his mother's Mountaineer. It was such a chick car, and on top of that, his only other choice was to hoof it wherever he needed to be during his supervised hours, as the judge had called it.

He could feel his mom watching him, and even though there was a bit of nagging conscience telling him she had once again saved his ass from serious trouble, Rodney couldn't make himself thank her out loud. He was sulking to the best of his ability, scowling, ignoring her attempts to reach him, and worse, he was irritated that he was actually feeling bad about his behavior.

"I cannot believe you left me in that place all night," Rodney finally muttered a few minutes later, as he slouched down even farther in the seat, pulling his blue knit cap down almost over his eyes.

"Rodney, there really wasn't any other way, especially since you needed to sober up." Susan knew there was no way Rodney would listen to her explanations, but she still wished she could get through to him.

Watching her from the corner of his eye, Rodney could see his mom trying to think of a new tact. He felt her nervousness about having to play warden, and there was a part of him that wished he could turn the clock back and make different choices.

Since that wasn't going to happen though, he'd have to make the best of where he was now in his life.

"So, what would you like for dinner tonight, honey?" his mom asked. She was trying to sound normal, as if everything was all right, but Rodney knew better.

"Bread and water is what they serve to prisoners in the old movies, isn't it, Mom?" Rodney snarled at her. "I mean that basically is what I am now, right? A prisoner in my own house?"

"Rodney, you know the judge offered you a great deal today. They could have kept you in jail until your charges came up for trial, or just sent you straight to that juvenile camp they were talking about. You don't belong in a place like that with all of those...hoodlums."

Rodney couldn't help but laugh when he heard this from his mom. "Mom, I'm one of those hoodlums, and I'm tough enough to handle whatever one of those little punks tries to throw my way!"

Instead of arguing with him, Rodney was shocked when his mother simply pulled the car over to the side of the suburban street they were driving down and parked next to the curb. Her hands tightly clenched the steering wheel, turning them almost white, and he could see the strain in her body. He braced himself for the lecture that was about to come his way, already planning some snappy comebacks aimed at hurting her when she tried to tell him what a good boy he could be if he'd just try to stay out of trouble.

Turning the car off, his mother turned and looked at him, and though there were tears in her eyes, Rodney also saw a look of steel. Sighing deeply, he heard words he'd never thought possible from his own mother.

"Maybe you're right, Rodney. Maybe you have become a hoodlum instead of the good person I raised you to be. You've made your own decisions, so maybe you do belong at the juvee center, and the judge has made a horrible mistake by letting you come home with me today. So, should we just turn around and go back, tell them there was a mistake, and you can leave as soon as possible for the camp?"

"Right, Mom, as if you would do that!" Rodney said with as much contempt and bravado he could muster. There was a small worry nagging at him that his mother wasn't bluffing, and an even larger doubt inside worrying she was right about him.

When he had first started experimenting with the drinking and drugs, it had been to escape the feelings he had about his dad. It seemed that the closer he got to puberty the worse all the stories that Taylor had told him started to make him feel. Maybe it really wasn't all because of his mom that his dad had left; instead, maybe he had left because he just didn't want to be a father to the new baby, Rodney.

Skipping school and getting high had made Rodney able to forget for a while how absolutely horrible he felt most of the time. Hanging out with Alan and Melinda let him share the hate he had inside. His mom had tried to take him to more counselors than he could remember, but Rodney had told her that psychologists were for crazy people, and he didn't want to be crazy.

He wanted to be tough and to keep people away from him. That made him pretty sure he wouldn't be getting hurt again, the way his dad's absence hurt him deep down in his gut. Going to school with a little buzz on made it easier to be brave and stand up to people. It was as if he were watching what he was doing and saying from somewhere high above his actual seat in the back of each classroom.

After a year of completely blowing off school, his grades had plummeted. He knew he'd have to pick it up at least a little or he wouldn't graduate. Plus, he needed to keep his mom off his back so he could have some freedom. By that point though it was harder to say no to the joint that got passed around at the bus stop or to the flask of vodka some stoner would have in the back of the locker room. It was also harder to remember the schoolwork that was presented. Rodney wasn't stupid, and he knew that if he failed high-school courses he'd be in summer school. However, he found his previous ease of memorizing wasn't there when he needed it anymore. He had started to freak out, worried that he may have actually cooked his brain cells without meaning to, just like that egg in the commercial.

"So, what's it going to be, Rodney?" he heard his mom ask again, breaking his reverie.

"I should just get out right now and take off," he yelled, grabbing the handle of the door and staring directly into his mother's face. Instead of crying or begging him to stay in the car, Rodney watched as his mother reached over and unlocked his door before sitting back in the driver's seat. Rodney flung the door open, but didn't move from his seat.

"Well, I guess that's your decision. If you get out, I will be forced to call Officer Reynolds and report you as a runaway. You'll be picked up and taken away from me. If you decide to be a man, and move on with your life in a positive way, then you can take your hand off the handle and stay in the car. That is what I prefer you choose to do, Rodney, but bottom line is, this time it is up to you."

Rodney was stunned, and even the cap pulled low over his face couldn't hide his shock from his mother's eyes. "You're telling me, that if I get out, you're not going to stop me?" he asked quietly.

"No, I can't stop you anymore, Rodney. I finally realize that ultimately it's your life. You're old enough to choose your path. So, I have to let you see what happens with those choices. You're not a baby anymore, even though when I look at you I can still see the little boy who used to let me snuggle him and read him bedtime stories. I can still hear your giggle when I would smother kisses all over the back of your neck. I will always love you more than I will ever be able to explain, but I can't keep fighting you, Rodney. I will help you however I can, but you need to do this for yourself this time. That's what I realized in the court today, sweetheart. This time it is up to you to make the right choices and get your life in line with what you want for your future."

Rodney listened to his mother's quiet tirade, and seeing the tears running down her face, he was ashamed for the first time he could remember in a very long time.

"So, Rodney, what's it going to be? Are you in, or are you getting out here?"

Rodney quietly pulled the door shut and sat back in the passenger seat. Without another word, his mother started the car and pulled away from the curb, checking carefully for traffic, and ignoring the wet tears marking her cheeks.

5

Once they arrived home, Susan silently handed Rodney his school bag with the accumulated lists of work he would need to make up while he was on his ten days of school suspension. "I'll make us some dinner, while you go and get started on this, okay?" she offered cheerily.

Suddenly too tired to fight, Rodney took the bag from her and walked upstairs to his room. Susan held it together until Rodney was out of sight, but then she collapsed onto one of the kitchen chairs and gave in to the shaking that overtook her frame. She could still feel the terror that had run through her soul in the ride home with Rodney. She had nearly been sick when Rodney had opened the door. What would she have done if he had actually gotten out and left her? She truly didn't know if she would've been strong enough to call Phillip and report her son if he had bolted.

The spasm passed, but left her feeling as if she'd just run a race without taking in enough electrolytes. Getting shakily to her feet, Susan moved to the refrigerator and took out supplies to make something passable for dinner. She loved to cook, but wasn't feeling very spunky at the moment.

Pouring herself a glass of white wine while perusing the kitchen, Susan decided that pasta would be good for both her and Rodney. Runners were always talking about "carbing up" before a big race, and she knew she and her son were going to need some energy to survive the next six months.

Susan was quickly lost in the world of culinary creations. The angel hair pasta boiled on the stove, and the scent of olive oil, butter, garlic, and mushrooms wafted from the skillet as she worked on a delicious sauce. There were no recipe books allowed in her kitchen in times like these. Unless she was baking something, she liked to mix and combine ingredients according to her own whims. Usually the results were well received, not that Rodney usually commented of course, but he had rarely left anything on his plate, even after taking second helpings. It was one small source of pride she took with her son, even during his most troubled times.

Draining the pasta in the colander, Susan watched the steam roll over the window above the sink, blanketing the dark autumn night with a fog that blocked her reflection. She stood silently for a moment, relaxing and taking a final sip of her wine. She decided to set the table as if for company, a small gesture to make sure that Rodney knew how glad she was that he was here with her tonight. Actually, if he followed the judge's plan, there would be an awful lot of family dinners in their future. She wasn't sure if that was a good thing yet, but she was pulling for positive things.

"It smells good in here, Mom," she heard the object of her good wishes say from the doorway.

"It does, doesn't it?" She laughed as she turned and handed Rodney the plates. Setting the silverware down on cloth napkins, she saw Rodney watching her from across the table.

"What?" Susan asked warily as Rodney grinned.

"You're using the fancy napkins." He laughed, reminding her of the private joke they used to throw around. She had taken both of her children to a rather upscale restaurant for a celebratory dinner when Taylor had graduated with honors from Oxford High School. Rodney had made an incredulous face when they were seated, holding out the cloth napkin to Susan and exclaiming that they must have been at a pretty fancy place, because they had napkins that weren't even made out of paper.

The waiter had chuckled and from then on, she and Rodney had joked about whether or not certain visitors or events were "fancy napkin worthy."

"Well, I think you are definitely worthy of the fancy napkins, Son," Susan said to Rodney. "Now, grab that basket of garlic bread and let's eat this food before it gets too cold to enjoy." She sat down and began to scoop out the pasta to Rodney, sending a silent thanks to Heaven for the blessings of surviving another day. She could only hope that it would be the first of many, and not the calm before the real storm broke on her life.

6

Rodney could tell that his mother was a nervous wreck the next day. She had to go to work, but was blatantly worried about leaving him at home during his suspension from school. Since he was being punished by the legal system the school had agreed to the minimum ten-day suspension, based on good behavior on his part. He and his mom had enjoyed a nice dinner the night before, but he found himself once again stressed out today, worrying about the judge's stipulations and terrified of the consequences if he failed.

He had tried to appear apathetic the night before when he threatened to get out of the car, but the truth was he wasn't as tough as he tried to act in front of everyone else. The tough guy façade was hard to keep up most of the time, but even more exhausting was the idea of letting it down for even a moment. If he let someone see weakness then he would become a target. He'd seen kids get beaten down for something as simple as smiling at a teacher or forgetting who was off limits on the quad outside of school.

When he had pulled his latest stunt, he'd been so high that the consequences hadn't occurred to him. However, when the judge discussed the Juvenile Detention Center, Rodney had felt waves of panic washing across him. He knew from talking to other kids who had served time in those places that they were basically a holding tank for kids too young to try as adults. Most of the kids there were major gang bangers and big-time criminals in the making. Sure, he could put on a big show, but he knew he'd be in over his head with the criminal elements there. He wasn't sure if he'd be able to make it out in one piece or even if he'd want to, if he were honest.

As he listened to his mother dash around her bedroom getting ready for work, Rodney felt the surge of power that rushed him when he knew he had the upper hand in a situation. Sure, his mom had sounded full of bravado the night before, but he knew how to push her buttons. He hadn't decided yet if he was going to try and play the game of good son to get her to fall into protective mode or just be a jerk and have her irritated and stressed out to throw her off her game. Maybe he would jump back and forth to keep her really off her feet, he was thinking as he rolled over in bed and brought the comforter over his head.

A loud knocking on his door interrupted his thoughts. This obviously meant that his mother was ready for work.

"Rodney," he heard her whisper rather gently outside the door. He knew if he just ignored her, she would eventually leave. When he decided to head downstairs somewhere around one or two this afternoon, he would find the usual note reminding him to have a good day and to be sure to eat the plate she'd left for him in the refrigerator.

"Rodney, time to get up, son," he heard this time. However, now she was in his room, and the door was ajar.

Looking up from his nest of blankets, Rodney tried first to pretend he was just waking up. "What is it, Mom? I'm super tired and not really feeling all that good," Rodney tried to explain in his best sick voice.

"Well, I'm afraid that's not really an option, honey," and with no pause in her answer she swept his blanket off the bed and turned on his overhead light, the one that was impossible to hide from as its glaring blast could unearth the dead.

"What are you talking about? I can't go to school. Remember? I'm suspended for ten days because that stupid prick principal won't cut me a break. Shocker, by the way, Mom, huh? That once again the pain-in-the-ass kid can't get a little slack from The

Man," Rodney tried, deciding to take the 'mama bear protecting her cub' approach. He figured, since they'd had a great time last night, he might as well use it and lull her into that false sense of security. She was always so eager to have him be the 'good little boy' she remembered from when he was a kid. It was easy to get his mom to forgive his transgressions and give him another chance.

"Yes, Rodney, I know, but the judge was pretty clear that you were not going to be laying about and having extra time on your hands, especially unsupervised time, if you recall?"

"So, what do you think, Mom? I'm not going to work with you at the flower shop!" Rodney was almost yelling now as he sat aghast, watching his mother rummage through his drawers and closet, throwing a way-too-clean pair of jeans and a couple of shirts onto his bed.

"Well, you would come with me to work if that was what the judge had decided, but that wouldn't be very much fun for either of us, now would it?" His mother sounded almost cheerful, and it was, in Rodney's opinion, way too early to be so perky. He simply sat in bed and glared, making the decision to try the silent treatment to get his morning person mother out of his room.

His mother just stood between him and the door of his bedroom, her arms folded akimbo in front of her, and smiled at him.

After what must have been a five-minute-long standoff, Rodney finally yelled, "So? What is this plan you have that obviously involves me getting out of bed at the butt crack of dawn?"

Laughing a little, his mother said, "First of all, it is hardly the butt crack of dawn, Rodney. Second, you are going to spend your ten days of suspension at the Oxford Youth Center. You have a big load of work to make up before you get back to high school. There are people at the center who can help you with all of that in between the times that they have you otherwise occupied. Think of it as a work-study program, honey," she added.

Rodney glared.

"We're leaving in fifteen minutes, so I'll go now so that you can get ready," and then she turned and almost skipped out of the room.

Rodney was floored. How dare they all assume that he'd just take off if left here alone. Sure, he might go and visit some friends, even though the stodgy judge seemed to think they were bad influences. Old people didn't know what the hell they were talking about most of the time. It was like all those crazy religious politicians who had tried to convince the public that music lyrics and video games were causing kids to be violent and stupid.

As he was contemplating how long he would have to ignore his mother before she just gave up and left him, she actually poked her head back through his doorway. Rodney was a little freaked out, as the two times his mother had been in his room this morning were more than she had been there in the last year put together.

"Oh, and son, if you're thinking of just ignoring me and defying my directions, then Officer Reynolds will be dropping by. Remember, your tether is programmed to keep track of where you are, like that GPS system you wanted. If you decide not to stick to the program and go to the Center, the judge will simply follow the agenda he explained to us yesterday in the courtroom."

As Rodney stared at his mom as if she were some alien creature, she added, "And to be honest, honey, I'd really like to have you around here a bit longer. I like having a reason to use the fancy napkins." She turned and left, yelling from down the hallway, "Ten minutes Rodney!" He could actually hear his mother whistling. Whistling? He wasn't sure exactly what the hell was going on here today, but he knew he needed to take back control of the situation pretty quickly.

Rising and getting ready to go, Rodney looked at his reflection in the mirror over his dresser. "You may have won this little skirmish, Mother, but I will win the war," he said out loud, playing the tough guy for his own benefit as he turned and left his room.

7

Susan made it down to the kitchen before she allowed herself to stop whistling and let out a panicky breath. It was usually Rodney that had her thrown, but today she had managed to break the pattern. She wished she could have seen his face as she'd started whistling. She knew herself well enough though to know that the sense of exhilaration and adrenaline she had felt when she left Rodney's room, hearing him actually get up and start to get ready, wouldn't last for too long.

Knowing from past experiences how this son and mother relationship worked, Susan was well prepared for the one step forward and then two steps backward flow of events with her and Rodney. As Rodney descended the stairs, Susan stood and picked up her bag and travel mug of coffee.

"All ready, sweetheart? Would you like some coffee and maybe a muffin to eat on the way? I made your favorite blueberry and banana coffee-cake muffins this morning."

Rodney had no response, but did reach out and snag two of the warm breakfast muffins as he stomped past her on his way out. Susan was fine with this. As long as Rodney was actually following the directions, she didn't care if he talked to her at all. She just wanted her son to find his way to a better path, and acting according to the judge's orders was a step in the right direction for Rodney. She'd let him act like the tough guy if it gave Rodney the out he needed in order to do as he was being asked.

Susan locked the house door, setting the alarm system as she left. Rodney's slumped form was already in the passenger seat, and she hurried to meet him. She knew they were running a bit behind. More importantly, though, Susan truly feared that if given too much time to think and fume over his current situation, her son would bolt and run as he had so many times in the past. She knew this time was more serious, and though she welcomed the assistance of the police given by the judge, it raised the ante for her son's behavior and consequences too.

Getting in quickly, Susan started the car. Before she drove away from the house, she could not resist turning to Rodney.

"Look, son, I know that this is a hard situation for you. I'm truly trying to help you, but like I said last night, this time it rests mainly on you and your actions. I will be here whenever you need or want my help, and I need for you to remember how very much I love you. I want this to be a good thing for you, Rodney. Just give it a few days and I think you'll see that things can get better, and easier for you if you just give it a chance to settle."

"Whatever, Mom," Rodney mumbled as he slouched down even farther into his seat. Pulling his hood down over his face, he added, "Can you just drive please so my hell can officially begin?"

Without another word, Susan did just that, giving her son the space she knew he needed. Aside from the sloshing of the coffee in her mug the car ride was silent. The radio remained off, which was an unusual occurrence as Rodney's first task usually was to blast her out of her thoughts with some horrible, heavy metal, hate-the-world station. Susan drove carefully, knowing that she was distracted, but even so, the short ride to the Center was quickly over.

She had expected Rodney to bolt before the car stopped next to the curb, but surprisingly he sat silent and still in his seat looking out at the white brick building. "Do you want me to go in with you today, honey?" Susan asked, quietly breaking the heavy silence of the car's interior.

"What? NO!" he answered in the surly tone she knew all too well from years of exposure to Rodney's disdain. Swinging his backpack onto his shoulder, he shoved open the door and jumped out.

As he began to walk up to the front door, Susan rolled down his window and yelled, "I'll pick you up at five o'clock Rodney!"

Rodney almost ran back to the car. "Mom, I am not an infant. I'll walk home when I'm done here at five o'clock. Even Judge Sphincter shouldn't have a problem with that, since he told me I'd be walking here after school every day for my community service hours. Besides, my tether will zap me or something if I go astray, right?"

"Rodney, the tether is not like an electric dog collar for Heaven's sake! It just lets the court know if you go AWOL until you get your act together." Susan was nervous about Rodney being on his own, but he was right. The judge had said he could walk here from school. "Fine then, son. I'll see you tonight at home. I love you, Rodney."

Without answering, Rodney spun on his heel and headed back up to the front of the building. Susan waited until he was all the way inside the double glass doors before she let out the breath she had unwittingly been holding. She tried not to count the number of days left before this phase of her life would be over, as it didn't seem like a very motherly thing to do. Besides, at this early stage of the game the remaining days stretched ahead of her like a marathon, and she had personally always felt that running was stupid. Filled with worry, she drove away, leaving her son to his day, trying to focus on the orders awaiting her at her shop.

8

odney stood in the front entryway, trying to decide whether he was going to stay or just take off and save everyone the trouble. The desk in front of him was unmanned, but there were noises in the background that gave evidence of people being close at hand. He was pretty sure he could hear the sounds of a basketball game going on, complete with the squeaking of shoes that his mother had always despised. Rodney had always loved the game of basketball, and had even played on the freshmen team in high school two years ago. By the time tryouts had come around during his sophomore year he had been ineligible because of grades and attendance issues. Plus, he'd become involved in other things with the bad influences the judge had mentioned.

Better things, he tried to convince himself, as he stood in the lobby listening to the muffled sounds of bouncing balls and the voices of competition. Deciding quickly that he'd had enough, Rodney began to turn around, and was stopped short by a laugh that came from behind him.

"Had enough already, huh, tough guy?" the voice said mockingly.

Ready for the inevitable confrontation, Rodney swiveled around and swallowed the retort he had prepared. The voice had come from the most beautiful girl Rodney had ever seen in his life. Standing only about five feet plus a few inches, her brown eyes laughed at him as she stood assessing him from a few feet away. Shaking her head in what was supposed to be dismissal, she turned around and moved to stand behind the desk.

Rodney didn't think he could take his eyes off the long, blond tresses, but then his teenage body was alerted to the firmness of her athletic form. Her warm scent drifted over him, and he actually closed his eyes to take a deep breath.

"Not sure what you're talking about, beautiful," Rodney answered when he finally noticed that she was staring at him waiting for him to say something.

"I'm talking about the fact that I watched you standing there thinking about whether to stay or go, and then head for the door," she said.

Rodney was smitten. He laughed out loud, denying her words with a vigorous shaking of his head. "No, I was just making sure that the door closed behind me when I came in," he explained in what he thought was his sexiest, most playful voice.

"Right," she said, shaking her head, which Rodney noticed caused her hair to sway enticingly against her collarbones. Rodney quite simply could not think about anything except how much he wanted to lean over the desk and kiss her skin right where the hair brushed her collar. Good God, what was wrong with him, he wondered.

"Mr. Rodriguez will be right out to explain how things work here," she said, totally ignoring Rodney's ogling. "You can sit down over there," she added, pointing to a row of hard plastic seats.

Rodney walked over to the desk, leaning on one elbow so that his flexed bicep was directly in her line of vision. "Who are you?" he asked, ignoring her directions.

Flipping her hair over her shoulder, she pointed to the official nametag pinned to her shirt that simply read, Veronica. Then she went back to work on the computer at the desk. Rodney just stood, watching her, until after a few minutes it became apparent that Veronica wasn't going to be making small talk with him. With a deep, theatrical sigh he slumped his shoulders and sadly dragged his feet over to one of the chairs. He sat down, dejectedly dropping his face into his hands, and began to stare at Veronica with a puppy dog expression.

After five minutes, she looked up and saw Rodney still watching her. Laughing, she muttered something that Rodney thought sounded like the word idiot, and went back to work. After another five minutes had passed, Veronica looked up again, and Rodney was still there, puppy dog affection clearly on his face.

Giving in, she laughed, clearly adding, "Idiot," much louder this time.

"Actually, it's Rodney," he said with a sigh. "I think I may be in love with you, Veronica, even though you are a cruel and heartless female," he added with a sadder expression than before.

Rolling her eyes, Veronica was saved from answering by the voice of Mr. Rodriguez yelling directions at someone as he walked down the hallway. Rodney stood as the short but powerful form of Director Rodriguez entered the room. "Ah, and you must be Rodney Birge, our newest addition to Oxford's Youth Center," he said with what seemed sincere welcome.

"Yes, sir, I'm Rodney," he answered. "Though I've been called worse very recently," he couldn't resist adding as he glanced over at Veronica.

She didn't look at him, but he saw her grin before pulling her face back into a serious expression and staring even harder at the computer screen.

"Well, let's go on back to my office and get you settled in, Rodney," Mr. Rodriguez said as he turned and walked away, knowing that Rodney would follow him down the hallway on the opposite side of the desk from which he'd entered. Rodney grabbed his backpack and swung it over his left shoulder, moving away from the lobby and into the depths of Oxford's Youth Center for the first time.

He couldn't resist a quick glance back to the desk. He was charged with a quick thrill as he saw Veronica looking at him, even though she looked away quickly when she realized she'd been caught. Rodney's face could hardly contain his grin as he walked behind Mr. Rodriguez.

9

Susan was deep in the arrangements for the Forrester wedding when she heard the ringing of the chimes that announced a client. Glancing up at the camera she had installed to have a view of the front while she worked, she was pleasantly surprised to see the uniformed Officer Reynolds entering, removing his hat as he did so.

Brushing her hands on the front of her apron, Susan made her way quickly to the front of the store. "Well, hello there," she greeted him. As he turned, she noticed the serious expression on his face and suddenly was engulfed in panic.

"Oh no, what has Rodney done?"

Phillip was at a loss. "What? I don't know. I haven't seen Rodney. Is he in trouble? Why didn't you call me, Susan?"

They both stood looking at each other, and as Susan realized her mistake, the tension left her body. "I'm sorry, Officer, I just assumed when you looked so serious, that something, well, all my instincts kicked in, and I just…"

"First of all, you agreed to call me Phillip. Second, you have no need to apologize for anything after all you've been through; and finally, I'm not here for any Rodney reason, so you can relax."

"Can you please wait here for just a moment then?" Susan asked. Without waiting for his answer, she turned and left.

Phillip stood where he was abandoned, somewhat abashed. He was still there, with a quizzical expression, as Susan entered, again brushing her hands on the front of her apron.

"Why, Phillip, what a nice surprise! What brings you to Floral Heaven this morning?" Susan reached out and shook his hand with both of hers, enjoying the sparkle of his hazel eyes when the small joke was realized.

He chuckled as they shook hands. He released her and began to meander around the showroom of her florist shop. "It's quite a bit bigger inside than the outside had me thinking," he commented, taking in the many different styles of vases and arrangements that Susan had on display. The colors and variety drew his eyes around the room in a purposeful way, and he was impressed, despite his limited knowledge of flora.

"Very nice, Ms. Birge, very nice indeed," he finally said out loud. He finished his perusal and ended up back in front of Susan.

Susan had stood still as Phillip explored. She wanted to watch him as he watched her shop. She knew that he was a trained observer, and she was curious whether or not her careful placements would carry his eyes as she had intended. Many of her customers simply hurried in, paid for preordered items, and left quickly. It seemed too many people were in a rush nowadays, and very few were willing to simply come in and enjoy. Susan could spend hours lost in the colors and scents of the bounty she worked with each day. Though Phillip hadn't spent a great length of time there, she had seen him absorb the path of flowers as she had intended.

"Well, thank you very much, Phillip, but you agreed to call me Susan as I recall," she couldn't help adding.

"So, how are you today, Susan?" he asked with sincere concern. "I didn't get a distress call, but that isn't always a great gauge of how the first night goes with folks."

"Actually, it went pretty well. He's at the Oxford Youth Center now, or at least he was seen walking into the establishment when I dropped him there this morning. Since I haven't gotten a call from anyone telling me his tether has been cut loose or is beeping his disappearance, I'm taking that as a good sign."

"One day at a time, as I always say," Phillip responded, twisting his hat in his hands.

"Would you like a cup of coffee?" Susan asked suddenly. "I was just brewing a fresh pot before you arrived."

"That would be very nice, Susan," Phillip said, following her into the back as she gestured to him. He was shocked as his senses were overwhelmed with the smells and colors of flowers in the workroom.

"How do you do this?" he asked Susan with wonder. "I barely know the difference between red roses and red carnations!"

"I've always been entranced with flowers and the power they have to create different moods," Susan tried to explain as she poured two large mugs of coffee. Motioning to the tray, she left Phillip's mug dark and black, pouring a large amount of flavored creamer into her own.

"Different moods?" Phillip asked as he took a careful sip of the hot coffee.

"Yes, each flower has the power to set a tone," Susan explained. "For instance, these large white daisies can lighten a room and bring joy just because of their size and good nature. The roses, well, there are so many variations of color and combinations with other types of flowers and greenery that their powers are almost limitless. Flowers are like people to me," Susan said.

"Flowers are like people?" Phillip said with a quirk of his eyebrow.

Susan watched his face above the large mug of coffee, seeing his eyebrow flicker in what seemed a gentle mocking.

"Yes, they are like people. Their behavior is somewhat dependent on who they're with at the time. For instance, my son?" She held up a single blood-red rose. "He gives off one mood when he is all alone." She illustrated by standing the flower in a tall, skinny vase by itself. "However, when he is with other kids who are also trying, just like him, to flip off the world, they feel like they have more power," and she added a large number of additional roses, all dark and almost dangerous.

"But, when my son tries to join a different group of what we might call good kids, he just doesn't seem to fit in," and she took the red rose and placed it in the middle of a group of large raspberry-colored peonies. She looked up and could see that Phillip was now listening with less humor and more understanding.

"What he doesn't seem to understand is that sometimes there are more than just those two options. It isn't always just good or bad, and there are ways to fit in with kids that aren't in the same family of trouble, so to speak, and still blend in without losing his individuality." As she had been talking, Susan had put together a bouquet of many different flowers, using the darkest rose, representing her troubled son, as one of the arrangement. The beauty of the flowers took Phillip aback. Though each of them was very different, the end result was stunning.

"That was incredible," he said when he finally took his eyes off of the large vase of flowers.

Laughing a bit self-consciously, Susan took a sip of her coffee. Putting the mug down, she moved to take the flowers out of the vase.

"What are you doing?" Phillip said, reaching out and stopping her with his hand gently around her wrist. "You just made that!"

"Yes, but it was just to show you what I was trying to explain." Susan laughed. "Now, I'll use the flowers for something more reasonable."

"I'll buy it," Phillip said suddenly, surprising himself.

"What?" Susan was shocked. She hadn't been trying to make a sale. The arrangement in front of her was beautiful, she had to admit, but it wasn't something she had intended on selling.

"Really, Phillip, there's no need for you to feel obligated to buy these flowers. It's not a big deal. I do this all day long, remember?"

"Yes, but I don't, and I suddenly realized that I need to have this. So, how much?" he asked, picking up the large vase and heading up front.

Susan rushed after him, all of the reasons she had to argue with him on the tip of her tongue. She watched as he set the vase down on the counter and took out his wallet. "And don't give me any discounted price either. I want these wrapped up like you would for a real customer and you charge me what you would anyone else." Phillip then put on his best cop face, giving her a look that must have convinced many people to listen to him and stop resisting.

"Phillip, I appreciate this, really, but this is a very extravagant arrangement in a very costly vase as well," Susan tried to explain.

"Well then, I'll compromise and take that good customer discount," he said without changing his expression as he handed her his credit card.

She couldn't help but laugh, and he smiled and relaxed. She had to give him credit when he didn't blanch even a little as he saw the total. She wrapped the flowers carefully with tissue paper, setting the vase itself into a sturdy box that fit snugly around it to prevent spilling during transport.

Phillip watched Susan as she readied the flowers for sale. She obviously loved her work, and that was important. He had simply come in to check on her. Seeing that she had something this important in her life would give her an outlet when Rodney got into trouble again, as he was sure Rodney would do before too much time had passed. He'd seen it all before, and though he tried to remain less than cynical, past experiences had taught him a lot.

Picking up his purchase, Phillip smiled at Susan. "I have to thank you," he said quietly to her. "I learned something new here today. I want you to know, that I'm rooting for your son. I hope he can figure out how to work well with others," he said as he pointed to the flowers he had purchased. "You are a breath of fresh air, Susan," he added as he swung open the door to the shop.

Susan watched Phillip leave her shop. She couldn't help but wonder if he was bringing the flowers home to someone he loved and cared about, or if he would simply donate them to the first place he came to during his day. He had seemed impressed with her work, but Susan had learned the hard way that people weren't always what they seemed. As she turned and went back into her workroom to finish the Forrester's wedding arrangements, she was shocked to acknowledge a bit of jealousy if there were a special someone about to receive the arrangement she had created. Pushing that thought away, she immersed herself in the comfort of her work.

10

Rodney had changed his mind about the Oxford Youth Center. It was as bad as he had thought. Mr. Rodriguez had quickly made it apparent that he was not going to be taken in by any of Rodney's tricks.

Clearly, the ten days of suspension were going to be spent in the exact opposite ways that Rodney had hoped when he had woken up that morning. There was a long list of chores that Rodney was going to be responsible for each day. Among this list were things like mopping the cafeteria floors, disinfecting the locker rooms, and making sure that any sudden spills or disasters were cleaned up as quickly as possible.

On top of the chores, there were the required hours of study hall. Mr. Rodriguez seemed to think that the time spent on his schooling should be seen as a blessing, but Rodney didn't agree. He wouldn't be able to make any time with Veronica if he were locked up with some stupid tutor, trying to relearn all of the math and history and English he'd blown off. So, Rodney had sat and listened to Mr. Rodriguez with a huge chip on his shoulder, ready once again to run from the building and cursing himself for not taking the out when he had a chance earlier in the day.

Rodney now found himself with a fresh bucket of disinfectant-laced mop water cleaning up the cafeteria for round two of lunches. He had been shocked to find out that there were permanent residents at the center, having assumed that it was more like a club for kids who just wanted a decent place to hang out. Mr. Rodriguez had explained that there were about twenty youths who lived there while awaiting their parents or guardians to get their lives straightened out enough to take their children back home.

Rodney didn't understand why the kids didn't just split and live on their own. Some kids he had seen were clearly old enough, though many were still pretty young. Even more shocking to Rodney were the smiles he saw on the faces of many of the kids he had been covertly watching as he mopped and cleaned throughout the morning. The poor little schmucks actually seemed like they were happy, which Rodney just couldn't get his mind around, knowing that to be here the kids' lives must have hit rock bottom.

Just as Rodney was finishing up the final round of the room with the dirty mop bucket, Mr. Rodriguez showed up out of nowhere. Motioning for Rodney to follow him, Rodney set the mop into the bucket off to the side of the room, where it wouldn't be in the way of the little feet. Rodney was shocked as he noticed the clock. It was already two o'clock.

They walked by the office, and Mr. Rodriguez had Rodney grab his backpack before they continued down the hall to a larger room, where there were smaller cubbies set up like a library study hall. Mr. Rodriguez motioned Rodney toward the back wall, where he waited for him to sit and place his bag on the desk.

"Now the hard work begins, young man," he said to Rodney. Rodney could feel the familiar panic set in as he worried about not being able to remember things that had once been so easy. He leaned forward in his chair, clenching his hands together in front of him, trying to maintain a cool demeanor.

Mr. Rodriguez placed a large stack of books and materials on the table near Rodney. "Your teachers put together all of the work you've missed while pursuing your 'other interests' shall we say?"

"Whatever," Rodney answered.

"That's 'whatever, Mr. Rodriguez,' son," Mr. Rodriguez said firmly. "Now, listen up. I know from your school records that you used to be quite a good student until you got involved with the wrong people and got into trouble. It's going to take some work on your part, but you can get back what you've lost if you're willing to try."

Rodney sat back and tipped his head to look up at Mr. Rodriguez. "No, I can't. It just isn't there anymore. I'm a lost cause, don't you get it?" Rodney had started out trying to sound tough, but his voice had risen an octave into fear and panic.

"Well, if you work at it with that attitude, you're right. You won't be able to fix anything, unless you decide to think about things with a positive attitude."

Rodney just sat and looked at this doubtful ally. "Why do you even care?"

Mr. Rodriguez sat down and looked eye to eye at Rodney. "Because I used to be where you're sitting right now, Rodney. I got involved in drugs, started skipping school, stole money from my own mother's purse, and ended up in the system. Just like you've done, right?"

Rodney sat quietly listening, but not giving any indication that he cared at all whether Mr. Rodriguez continued or not with his story. Mr. Rodriguez huffed and said, "Oh, I know, you're thinking 'so what' or that I'm making this all up to get close to you." In order to prove his point, Mr. Rodriguez pointedly rolled up his left pant leg to show the black gang tattoo. "But that is not what is going on here, Rodney."

"So, you were in a gang, and you were a bad ass. Is that what you want me to understand?" Rodney spat the words, letting all his frustrations boil over his shaky persona of tough guy.

"No, Rodney, what I want you to understand is that even with all of the people who believe in you, your life won't change until you can believe in yourself."

The two men sat looking at each other until Rodney dropped his gaze and looked out of the window on the far side of the room. With a deep sigh, Rodney reached across and took a book and folder off the top of the pile Mr. Rodriguez had set down.

It was his math curriculum, and math had always been his strongest subject.

"So, does that mean you're willing to give this a good try, Rodney?" Mr. Rodriguez asked.

"Sure, though I'm not sure how much of this is still somewhere in my brain," Rodney said, leafing through the pages.

"Well, I never said you were going to have to do this alone, Rodney," said Mr. Rodriguez. As if there had been a silent signal, the door opened, and into the study center walked Veronica. Along with a stack of books, she carried two bag lunches.

"Hey," Rodney said to her with another unusually large smile.

"Hey," Veronica answered, sitting down and nodding to Mr. Rodriguez. She handed Rodney one of the bags. "Tomorrow, you can eat in the cafeteria, but I thought we'd need all of our time to get started today," she explained.

"Well, I'll leave you to the capable and knowledgeable services of Miss Veronica," Mr. Rodriguez said as he stood up to leave. "Remember, Rodney, before you worry about letting anyone else down, first think about the seriousness of letting yourself down."

Mr. Rodriguez left then, and Rodney took a deep breath and sat back in his chair. "Whew, that was close." He laughed as he turned to look at Veronica.

"Close? What are you talking about?" Veronica asked as she took another notebook out of the pile. "Let's get to work, Rodney," she said.

"Are you serious? But he's not even here," Rodney added incredulously as Veronica continued to set up the small study area.

"No, but I am, and if you were planning on being a slacker, you would have been better off if Mr. Rodriguez had stayed instead of me. I'm earning Honor Society points for tutoring, plus I volunteer at the desks before school some days when Mr. Rodriguez needs me. So, turn around and let's get busy."

Rodney simply stared. When Veronica began to review the algebraic equations in front of them, he shook his head in disbelief. "So, out of the pan and into the fire, as the saying goes, huh?" He laughed.

"Rodney, you aren't even going to know what's hit you!" Veronica laughed as she passed him another sharpened pencil. "Now, let's get busy."

Three hours later, Rodney was shocked to find Mr. Rodriguez standing over them. "Time to go, Rodney," he said. "Five o'clock ends your duty time."

Rodney stacked up his papers and carefully put them into a pile. "Should I just leave all of this here, Mr. Rodriguez, or take it somewhere else until tomorrow?" Rodney asked.

"So, you're planning on coming back again, Rodney?" Mr. Rodriguez asked.

Rodney laughed as he stood and swung his backpack onto his shoulder. "Like I have a choice, right?"

"There's always a choice, Rodney," he said as Rodney passed him.

Rodney scowled and walked away without looking back to see the man's reaction. One day was down but many were ahead of him. He couldn't help but wonder what Melinda and Alan had been up to as he'd sat here all day working.

Walking away from Oxford Youth Center, Rodney felt the positive feelings that had sprouted begin to fade. He wasn't sure how long he would be able to keep ahead of the crew he needed to leave behind in order to meet the judge's requirements.

11

Susan had arrived home earlier than usual in order to create a special meal for Rodney on his first day of suspension at Oxford Youth Center. She had set the table with linen napkins and the best china. The crystal bowl held the Caesar salad that was Rodney's favorite. In the heated dish were red potatoes roasted in olive oil with an assortment of spices that Rodney used to find irresistible and the carrot puff casserole that he used to think was actually a dessert instead of a vegetable. The thick steaks awaited his appearance so she could grill them to his preferred medium rare on the preheated grill outside on the patio.

She'd prayed off and on all day that Rodney had actually stayed at the center. She hoped he would make it home on time, so that there would be no problems with the tether. Though she hated the idea of her baby boy having to wear such a device, she had to admit that it gave her some peace of mind. Knowing that someone would know immediately if her son made a sudden stupid choice had allowed her to get a good night's sleep and also rest easier while she had been at work during the day.

It was almost 5:30 when she heard Rodney come in the front door. They usually used the back door off the kitchen, but she guessed her son might need a minute to himself instead of walking right into his mom today. She went ahead and put the duo of thick steaks onto the hot grill. As she reentered the room, she saw Rodney reaching out to snag a bite of salad. Leaning against the doorway, Susan cleared her throat loudly, raising an eyebrow at the acceptable thievery of her son.

"Sorry, Mom, I couldn't resist," Rodney said as he dropped a large mouthful of greens into his mouth. Susan laughed and walked over to hug her son.

"I'm so glad you're home, honey. How did it go today? Was it okay?" Susan asked, moving about the kitchen and watching the steaks as they grilled, sending a delicious scent into the fall air.

"Fine. How long until dinner?" Rodney answered vaguely.

"Under ten minutes, so you'll have time to go and put your things away and wash up if you'd like," Susan answered. She was disappointed that Rodney seemed so unwillingly to share, but also wasn't terribly surprised. Trying to get information from a sixteen-year-old boy was sometimes more work than it was worth. Susan knew that she would have to settle for the "no news is good news" outlook. Plus, she had her secret source of information, Phillip, if she felt the need to dig further.

A short time later, she and her son sat around a quiet table enjoying the steak dinner with the fancy napkins. She watched Rodney pick up his napkin and place it across his lap before he dug into his plate. Susan smiled at him, knowing that at least one lesson taught when he was young had stuck. She, Taylor and Rodney used to have special evenings when all three would dress in their finest and pretend to be in different amazing places around the world. Sometimes, they were at a European castle or India's Taj Mahal. There were Japanese garden parties and teas with the Queen of England that had been hosted by Susan for her children. They were some of her best memories, and recalling them now made her miss her oldest, twenty-four-year-old Taylor, sharply.

"We should call Taylor and have her come home for a visit soon," Susan thought out loud, glancing at Rodney as she did.

"Tired of dealing with me alone already, Mom?" Rodney asked, tossing down his knife and fork and reaching for another slice of crunchy bread.

"Not in the least, Rodney, which you know for a fact," Susan said softly. "I was just thinking of our 'dinner parties' and how nice it would be to have both of my children together for a little while."

Rodney continued eating, and Susan used his preoccupation to observe her son. He had changed so much since he was just a boy, but the underlying lack of self-esteem and mild jealousy of his sister seemed to lurk somewhere deep inside of him. Part of it, she knew, came from Rodney's belief that Taylor had been gifted with more time with their father. Of course, Rodney had been too young to know what his father had truly been like when they had all been together. Therefore, Rodney's mind was free to paint a picture of the perfect family. To this day, Susan knew Rodney doubted the facts she had told him about why his father wasn't with them anymore.

Along with the whole daddy issue, Susan also knew that Rodney resented Taylor's success in school. She could still remember the fights that had started as Rodney, even though he was so much younger, would comment about how easy it was for Taylor. Taylor had always done well in school, but it was because she had studied hard and taken each academic situation as a challenge to be met. Taylor was old enough during the rough times to remember the taunting her father used to throw at them. Whether Taylor had pushed herself so hard to prove him wrong, or simply to ensure that she never ended up like him, Susan didn't know. But, Taylor had decided at a very early age to graduate at the top of her class, go on to an outstanding university, and get a job somewhere far away from Oxford City, Connecticut. Not that New York City was horribly far away, but in terms of the character of the places, it was an entirely different world.

Rodney had continued eating during Susan's musings, but Susan could see the tension playing around his clenched cheeks. "It has been a long time since Taylor came home for a visit, Rodney." Susan tried to broach the subject again gently.

"Yeah? Well whose fault is that, Mom?" Rodney's retort came with the emphasis of slicing into the thick steak in front of him with more vigor than necessary.

"Well, I would like to have her here if she can manage it. Plus, I'm feeling the mood to cook both of my children's favorite meals," Susan added playfully.

At this, Rodney looked up and actually grinned. "Oh, well, in that case, I would love to have my older sister for a visit," he said. "And, before you ask, of course it isn't just because her favorite meal is prime rib and all the fixings," he added, laughing out loud.

"Well, I'm glad to hear that, Rodney, especially since the last time I talked to Taylor she told me that her favorite meal is now some crazy tofu stir-fry," Susan said. Rodney's face turned a shade of green, and Susan laughed. "I'm kidding!" She chuckled.

"Geesh, give me a heart attack, Mom," he coughed. "Tofu? Not even Taylor could have changed that much in the six months since I've seen her last!" he added.

"Oh, six months is it? I thought you didn't remember how long it had been since Taylor had been here?" Susan smiled gently. She knew that despite Rodney's efforts to deny his lack of feelings for Taylor, there was an underlying love and need for her approval.

"Pass the carrots, please," Rodney answered in order to ignore Susan.

"Glad you're enjoying the meal," Susan offered up in a subtle change of subject. "There's chocolate ice cream for dessert," she added. "You can have it now, or wait until later if you'd like, Rodney."

"How about if I try a bowl now, and then maybe have another one later, too?" Rodney suggested.

"I don't think that would be a problem at all," Susan said, wishing that an extra bowl of ice cream could be Rodney's only issue over the next few months. She had worried all day, and now the fears were encroaching again on her thoughts.

"So, are you going to tell me anything about your day at Oxford Youth Center?" she asked as she got up to get the ice cream from the freezer.

"Nothing to tell. They made me work like some stupid janitor and then made me study. Then I came home."

Susan scooped out a large dish of chocolate ice cream, not giving into the deep desire to beg Rodney for more information. She had known that this time around was going to be the toughest of all. Rodney was either going to accept her offerings of listener and advocate, or he would block her out as he had so many other times.

"Sounds really nice, Rodney," she said, setting down the bowl and a clean spoon in front of him. Without another word, Susan started to clear off the dinner table, scooping the small bit of leftovers onto a divided Tupperware plate for her lunch tomorrow, if it survived the night with Rodney lurking through the refrigerator. As she began to wash the dirty dishes, Susan refused to ask Rodney anything more about the center. She needed to stick to her guns this time, even if it meant swallowing all her instincts to protect her heart from being broken once again by her puzzling teenage son.

Susan felt Rodney approach the sink, setting his empty bowl on the counter next to where she stood looking out at the grill and their backyard that was transforming into fall.

As Rodney turned to walk out of the room, Susan called his name. She felt him tense.

"Yeah?" he answered, and Susan could see the smug look on his face as he turned, clearly telling her that he knew she wouldn't be able to resist the need to dig into his day.

"Can you turn the grill off for me, please? The residue should have burned off by now, and I don't want to forget and leave it on again."

The smug look was replaced by confusion. Rodney walked out and did as Susan had asked without another word.

Good, Susan thought. She knew it was important that Rodney understand that this time was different for both of them. Susan had always been clear with her son, making sure he never had a real reason to doubt that she loved him more than anything in the world. However, she had also always tried to be consistent and not give in to the childish cries of how mean she was when she enforced consequences for poor choices.

Susan was just finishing rinsing the last dish as Rodney came back inside the house. "Thanks," she said, laying the dishtowel across the rack to dry. With a grunt, Rodney walked away and made his way upstairs to his room. As he moved out of sight, Susan allowed herself to slump against the countertop. Though she was firm in her resolve, it was exhausting to always be on guard with her own child.

Looking forward to a hot bath and a few chapters of the mindless novel awaiting her upstairs, Susan locked up the house and made her way to her own room. As she passed Rodney's room, Susan listened, but all she heard was the brain-numbing music her son loved.

She knocked softly on his door, and the music went mute. "Good night, son," Susan said to Rodney through the closed door.

"'Night," he said, and the music immediately went back up in volume. Susan placed her hand gently on the door, palm flat, fingertips pressed in, wishing she could make everything right. She wouldn't wish to turn back the clock, because she really didn't know what she would do differently if given another chance. That was the frustrating part for her, the not knowing. Rodney had simply taken one wrong turn after another, fighting her each step along the way. Once he began to experiment with the drugs, Susan had known she was losing the fight to save her son from his demons.

Silently pulling her hand off the door, Susan sighed and made her way into her room. She would melt away her stress in an almost too-hot tub of water, lose herself in the vapid romantic dilemmas of the heroine of the novel and try to forget all about the juvenile detention system for the rest of the evening.

12

Rodney had returned the next day to the Oxford Youth Center, and the next and the next. Each day followed the same pattern, and Rodney grudgingly admitted to himself that he had begun to look forward to being there. Since there were some permanent residents, Rodney had even been able to be there on his weekends. Even though he would never share the information with his mother, Rodney was relieved that all of his time was being taken up with his community service hours. He was clean for the longest stretch of time he could remember and had zero opportunity to get into trouble. Between Veronica's severe tutoring and Mr. Rodriguez's overseeing duties, Rodney was actually feeling some pride in his abilities.

Today was his last day of full-time community service, since tomorrow he would have to return to Oxford High School for the first time since his arrest. Rodney was nervous as hell and worried that he'd still be so far behind in classes that all of his hard work wouldn't make any difference. Though he had tried repeatedly to get Veronica to treat him as more than a pupil, she had shown no interest in any romance. Rodney had finally given up and told her he would have to settle for just being friends, until she came to her senses of course. Veronica had laughed and told Rodney she would be honored to have him as a friend. Her sincere smile had caused Rodney's stomach to flip, but he had maintained his cool demeanor and not let on how much he really liked her.

One great thing about being at Oxford Youth on the weekends was that he didn't have to put in any study time. He spent his mornings playing janitor, but in the afternoons he had earned the opportunity to either study or use the facilities. Rodney had found some guys to play pickup basketball games with last Sunday, and he was looking forward to another few hours on the court this afternoon.

As he was putting away the mop bucket and other cleaning supplies from his morning routine, he caught his reflection in the mirror on the back of the door. From the outside Rodney knew people saw just a surly punk; but if they would only give him a chance, Rodney thought he could be better. Talking to the counselor at Oxford had almost been helping, Rodney thought, as he brushed his shaggy hair from his eyes. The guy seemed to know what Rodney was thinking without having the right words to explain. He didn't push Rodney to share like his mother was always trying to do or at least like she used to try.

That was one thing Rodney had told the counselor, Mr. Oakes, a few days ago. His mom used to always be on his case about telling her everything, but this time around it seemed like if Rodney didn't answer, his mom just let it drop. It was really starting to piss him off too. When Rodney said this, Mr. Oakes actually laughed.

"Rodney, she's all done playing games with you. You had to know that at some point your sullen behavior would cause this situation, right?" Mr. Oakes explained.

"What the hell are you talking about?" Rodney shot back at the counselor. "She's my mom, and she's supposed to be trying to help me, not being a bitch about things."

"So tell me how your mom is 'being a bitch' about things Rodney," Mr. Oakes asked without blinking at Rodney's use of profanity. "She has taken on the responsibility given to her by the court after your last stunt at school. She has driven you here each day, making sure that you are where you're supposed to be on time. She has provided you with a safe place to live and great meals if I'm to believe what you've been telling me. Plus, now when you give her grief about not prying, she has done just that and backed off and left you alone."

Rodney slumped back in his chair during Mr. Oakes's recap. "Have I summed your mother's behavior up fairly accurately, Rodney?"

Sitting up just a bit, Rodney nodded toward Mr. Oakes. A number of minutes passed before either of them said anything else.

"So, what part of that list could label your mother in the manner you have described, young man?" Again, Rodney didn't answer. Finally, he sighed, and looked up at Mr. Oakes, who was still watching him intently.

"Well, it still pisses me off," Rodney said, not able to admit that he was wrong.

"Basically, what you're telling me, Rodney, is that according to you, your mother is damned if she does what you want and damned if she doesn't do what you want."

Almost so quietly that Mr. Oakes was unable to hear him, Rodney replied, "Yeah, but isn't she supposed to love me no matter what I say?"

"Oh, Rodney, your mother loves you more than you will ever be able to understand. At least, you won't understand until you have a child of your own to take care of in the future." Mr. Oakes leaned forward and placed a hand on Rodney's shoulder. "Have you ever taken a moment to consider how hard it is for your mother to back off and not ask you a million questions? Or, how hard it must be for her to simply drop you off here and then wait at home until you return, while she gets to wonder every minute of the day whether or not you're doing what you're supposed to be doing?"

Rodney pulled his pant leg up to expose the GPS tether to Mr. Oakes. "Well, she does have some handy help in that department, doesn't she?"

"Rodney, you brought that tether on yourself, and you know that perfectly well," the counselor calmly retorted. "It was either that, or juvenile detention, and quite honestly, based on your record, Judge Garcia didn't need to give you another chance. He did that based on the knowledge that you have a strong parent at home willing to assist in your recovery. He gave you the extra chance based on the feedback from Officer Reynolds. He gave you one more try to turn your life around Rodney, and from what I have seen, you have done a fine job so far of taking advantage of this opportunity to the best of your ability." Mr. Oakes finished firmly, letting the compliment sink in as Rodney's brain processed this.

"What?" Rodney said, surprise clearly written all over his face.

"I said, nice job young man." Mr. Oakes stood and stretched his arm out to shake Rodney's hand. Rodney stood, putting himself on equal ground with the counselor, and stretched out his arm as well.

"Thanks," Rodney said.

"Good luck on Monday, Rodney. Don't let all of this hard work be for nothing; and remember, I will be here to listen and help you with things for as long as you need me."

Rodney left Mr. Oakes's office that afternoon feeling both elated and terrified. He had almost forgotten then about the inevitable Monday return to school, and now it was only a short half-day away. Shaking the hair out of his eyes again, Rodney pulled himself out of his daydreaming, pulling the sweatband on with the mirror's assistance. A few hard hours of basketball should help loosen the tight band of fear that was gripping his heart and bowels. If nothing else, he knew his body was in the best shape of his life. Now, if he only felt the same way about his mind and what little remained of his soul.

13

Since Rodney was spending his weekends at the Youth Center, Susan had taken advantage of her free Sunday to take a walk through the paths in the nearby nature area. She was seriously stressing about Rodney's return to school the next day, and a quiet, solitary walk was just what the doctor ordered.

The well-maintained crushed gravel paths led Susan gently uphill through stands of pines and hardwoods. Sunlight penetrated the trees in some places and created random areas of warmth. Fall wild flowers poked out here and there adding dots of purple and white to the forest floor.

Susan found her mind wandering from her fears about Rodney's current delicate balance and back to the final months of her marriage to Rodney's father. After she had discovered her pregnancy and decided to stay with Joe, things had leveled out for a short time. Joe had stayed sober and had even found a new job that helped with the bills that had accumulated.

• • •

Of course, once Rodney had been born, the additional costs of diapers and formula had begun to take their toll and Joe began to stay out later after work to have a beer or two with the guys. Susan would come home from work and, after picking the kids up from Mrs. Arlen's house, she would try to pretend that things were not spiraling downward once again.

As Susan finished putting the kids to bed one night, she came out and found Joe standing in the front door, the telltale fumes of the local bar hovering around him. Trying to behave as if everything were fine, Susan smiled and started picking up the toys in the living room.

Joe slammed the front door, weaving as he sauntered into the room. "What's for dinner?" Joe finally asked, as he flopped onto the couch and flipped on the television.

"I have a plate from dinner that I can warm up for you, Joe. It's your favorite, my special meat loaf and mashed potatoes," Susan answered. She moved quickly to heat it up, hoping that Joe would be asleep by the time she returned.

As she moved to the couch, Joe's eyes closed, and Susan breathed a sigh of relief. But as she put the plate down on the table, Joe sat up and snatched her wrist in his tight grip, pulling her down onto his lap.

"How about you show me a little appreciation for a hard day at work?" he slurred, clumsily grabbing at Susan and trying to kiss her.

Knowing better than to tell him no, Susan tried to distract him instead. "Don't you want to eat your dinner before it gets cold, honey?"

Joe wrapped his arms tightly around Susan's arms, so that she couldn't move away from him. Susan always tried to keep the fear off her face, as it seemed to fuel Joe's behavior. This time, however, she couldn't, and she saw his face flicker with twisted desire. A maniacal smile spread over his face, and he leaned in and kissed Susan hard, drawing blood.

Susan hardened her body, willing Joe to stop his attack. The smell of whiskey was overpowering, and Susan fought against the urge to be sick. Joe moved to her neck, biting in order to get some type of response. She knew that when he was like this, his need to control her reactions was the spark he wanted.

"Not into it tonight, huh, babe?" Joe snarled, pulling back and looking at Susan.

Susan decided to try another tact, and using all of her reserves, said sweetly, "Joe, you know how much I love you, but I made you this beautiful meal, and I wanted to have a special dinner when you got home." Her husband looked at her, his drunken mind trying to process her words. Susan thought she might be in the clear and that was when she heard the children's bedroom door open.

The soft patter of footed pajamas was clear on the wood floor, and then Taylor was standing next to them, holding Rodney's hand. Rubbing her eyes sleepily, Taylor smiled at Joe. "Hi, Dad! Baby Rodney needed a drink of water."

Joe sat rock still, his breathing still coming hard and fast. Clenching his teeth, he surprised Susan when he answered rather calmly, "Well hi, little girl. What a nice surprise to see you. Daddy had to work late, and I was afraid you two would already be too sleepy to see me tonight." Susan was shocked once again that Joe was able to lie so smoothly and quickly, even when drunk.

Taylor smiled at Susan, and Susan realized that Taylor was faking this whole incident. Rodney had clearly been dragged out of bed, barely awake on his feet. Thankfully, Joe was too drunk to notice, but Susan and Taylor understood each other's protective behaviors. Susan was awash with guilt, as she realized that her young daughter had needed to develop survival skills in her own home.

"Can Mommy get you a drink of water?" Susan asked Taylor and Rodney, not looking back to Joe, who still had a death grip on her body.

"Wanna go bed," Rodney's baby voice piped in suddenly, as he rubbed his sleepy eyes.

"Okay, baby," Susan said. "Mommy will take you back to bed."

Joe's grip tightened just enough that Susan had to fight a gasp of pain. "Taylor, you can take Rodney back to bed, right, honey?" Joe said softly.

He released Susan and stroked a finger gently down Taylor's cheek. "Mom and I are having a little dinner together, and I just don't want to let her go because I love her so much," Joe said.

Susan saw that Taylor didn't want to leave her. She also knew this needed to end soon or Joe would lose it. This situation could get dangerous for her children very quickly.

"Mom?" Taylor said softly. "Can you get me a drink first?"

"Taylor, go get a glass of water if you need one," Joe snapped. Susan nodded at her, and as Taylor led Rodney into the kitchen Joe leaned forward. Whispering dangerously into her ear, Joe played out his most popular threat.

"If you don't stop fighting me, I am going to take those two kids and disappear. You will never find me, and you will never know what happened to them. It's an awfully dangerous world we live in now Susan, and God only knows what could happen to such sweet, innocent children. You got it?" He grabbed her breast for emphasis.

"Yes, Joe, I've got it," Susan said, a sob catching her voice.

Taylor and Rodney came back, and Susan smiled and told Taylor it was time for bed.

"It's okay, baby. I'll see you in the morning," Susan said, trying to ease her daughter's fearful expression. "I love you."

"I love you too, Mom," Taylor said.

"What about me? Don't you love me, too?" Joe said to Taylor.

Taylor only hesitated for a moment before she answered, "Yes, I love you, too." Before she shut the door, Taylor looked at her mother one more time. Susan gave her daughter the bravest smile before mouthing the words, "It's okay," and then the door shut.

The room filled with silence. Susan sat motionless, praying against all hope that Joe was too drunk to finish what he had started or would simply lose interest, having won the control battle.

"Now, where was I?" he said quietly as he dragged her off the couch and pushed her toward their bedroom.

"Joe, please," Susan tried one more time.

"Yeah, that's it Susan. Beg me for it," he sneered, shoving her harder toward the bedroom.

Susan could not stop the tears that began, knowing that if she fought her husband he would make sure she paid dearly. If she simply gave in, he would at least finish quickly, and Susan didn't want Taylor to hear what was about to occur. Without another sound, Susan turned and went into the room. She undressed quickly and lay under the sheet, listening to Joe's threats as he stripped and crawled on top of her.

Her children were the most precious things in the world to her, and Susan would do whatever it took to protect them. She blocked out Joe's pinches and grunts, planning how she could manage to protect Taylor and Rodney from their own father. As Joe finished, rolling off of her still form to pass out beside her, Susan knew that the two-year remission was at an end. She had known it wouldn't last, but had prayed to be wrong this time.

Susan silently cried herself to sleep, finding her thoughts leading time and again to dead-end solutions to her situation. She had no money, two little kids, and no family to rely on for help. Despite this, she knew she had to do something.

• • •

The snapping of a dried out branch brought Susan out of her reverie. Shaking off the memory, she realized her walk had taken her far up into the hills of Connecticut, and when she reached the overlook area, she took advantage of the peace and quiet, curling up on one of the benches supplied by the Connecticut Parks Department. Pulling a small throw out of her backpack along with a bottle of water, Susan took in the beauty surrounding her. She had come a long way since that painful time in her life fourteen years ago.

"Time is supposed to heal all wounds," she said to the squirrels chittering in the red and golden treetops above her head.

"Well, that's what they say," she heard from her left. Susan jumped about a foot as she leaped up in surprise, dropping her water bottle and watching it roll under the two-railed fence, a mild barrier to the steep decline in front of her. As she listened to the bottle bouncing down the side of the hill, Susan turned to see Phillip standing before her.

He was dressed in casual denim jeans, and she could see a soft cotton shirt of burnt orange underneath the open buttons of a flannel shirt. His sleeves were rolled up to midelbow, and Susan's eye was drawn to the strength of his arms.

"Well, surprise," she heard him say. "I'm so sorry to have startled you!"

"Are you stalking me, Officer Reynolds?" Susan asked. When he looked at her with an admonishing raised eyebrow, Susan corrected herself. "Sorry, are you stalking me, Phillip?"

His deep laugh echoed down the valley in front of them, and Susan couldn't help but laugh with him.

"Actually, I walk here every Sunday, rain or shine," Phillip explained. "So, maybe you're the stalker, huh?" He softened the joke with a smile, taking in Susan's mutually casual dress of jeans and soft gray zippered sweatshirt.

"The only thing stalking me these days seems to be bad memories," Susan said out of the blue, turning back to look at the view.

"Are things bad with Rodney, Susan?" Phillip asked, moving closer to her.

"No, actually things have been pretty good; but he goes back to school tomorrow. I know he's nervous, but he won't share anything with me. He's been doing great at the center, as far as I can tell; and even more importantly his drug drops have shown him to be clean and sober. But..." Susan added.

"But, you've been there and done this before? You're afraid to get your hopes up? You want to follow him to school and fight off anyone who is mean or harmful to your baby?" Phillip said in a rush of possible explanations.

Susan turned back to Phillip and laughed. "Yes, all of the above." She reached for her water bottle, and then remembering where it was said, "You cost me a water, stalker!"

Phillip tried for a look of shameful, abashed innocence, but didn't quite pull it off. Without thinking twice, he offered, "So, why not let me buy you lunch? A nice meal accompanied by a decent glass or two of wine?"

Susan was surprised. She was sure that Phillip had someone to spend time with, and that whomever it was would not appreciate his taking her to lunch. As she hesitated to answer, Phillip jumped in to reassure her.

"No strings attached, Susan. Besides, I'd like to hear about Rodney's success of the last two weeks. His tether hasn't alerted to any type of violation and that's very rare. Of course, not many of the minors I work with have such a support system in their mom, either."

"I am a bit hungry," Susan admitted, picking up her bag. "Somewhere casual though," she said, gesturing to her style of dress.

"I know just the place," Phillip said, pointing to his own jeans and flannel shirt. Holding out his elbow in a gentlemanly fashion, he said, "May I?"

Susan couldn't resist smiling as she tucked her hand into his elbow. She felt her fingers warm in the crook of Phillip's arm, as they made the twenty-minute walk to the parking area in silence. Giving her directions to follow him in her own car, Phillip gently escorted Susan into the driver's seat of her vehicle. She found herself smiling in anticipation of a meal with another adult.

In no time at all, she was pulling up behind Phillip's pickup truck into the parking lot of a log cabin-styled establishment, about ten miles or so outside of Oxford. The two-story building was large, but had a cozy appeal to it, with a huge wraparound porch. The view was breathtaking, and Susan stepped from her car and instantly took a deep breath of the aroma of autumn leaves and cool, fresh air.

"Here we are, as promised," Phillip said, walking around to lead her onto the porch. "This is one of my favorite places, especially this time of year." Pushing open the large door, Susan stepped into a scene from the past. The inside was decorated like a hunting lodge from earlier times. There was a massive fireplace in the center of the room, and mounted trophies of deer, elk, moose, and even a bear were hung all around the room's perimeter.

"I hope it's not too 'dead animal décor' for you?" Phillip asked, as he walked past the please-seat-yourself sign and led Susan to a small table near the fireplace and the large paned window that looked out into the forest beyond.

"This is perfect," Susan honestly exclaimed. Connecticut was a beautiful state, and Susan had chosen Oxford for its seclusion and the security offered by the small town's independence. Places like this were a balm to her battered soul, and a sigh escaped her as she sat in the cushioned seat Phillip pulled out for her.

"Are you really okay, Susan?" Phillip asked as he took his own seat and nodded at the waiter who softly approached their table.

"How nice to have you with us today," said the surprisingly well-spoken young waiter who introduced himself. After a few moments spent browsing the menu and getting a bottle of wine, Phillip explained to the waiter that they planned on a very relaxed afternoon. So, for now, they would be talking and enjoying the wine, and that he would call the server over when they were ready to order. The waiter nodded, taking it all very seriously, and then Phillip looked at Susan and asked her again how she was doing at home with Rodney.

"Well, I meant what I said earlier. He really does seem to be making better choices lately. For some reason though, I keep having flashbacks and horrible dreams about Rodney's future. I don't know what to do, and I feel ridiculous even saying it out loud." Susan ended rather desperately.

"Do you want to talk about it?" Phillip asked, pouring them both a large glass of wine, a specialty red from the local vineyards.

"Yes, I'm sure that's exactly how you want to spend your day, right? Listening to the frantic tale of a woman who was too stupid to leave her husband when he first hit her, and who stayed for years trying to make things work out for the stereotypical reason of 'doing what's right for the children' but instead puts them into even worse danger." Unable to look Phillip in the eyes, she chose gazing into the heated bricks of the fireplace instead.

Phillip didn't say a word, and Susan felt his hand rest softly over the top of her own as it clenched on the table. At first, Susan continued her fire watching, but when she felt Phillip calmly squeeze her hand, she turned and looked him fully in the face.

"Tell me," he said. "I will sit here and listen. I will not judge. I will fill your wine glass and be a keeper of your secrets, Susan. You need this."

"I don't even know where to start," Susan said.

"What were you thinking about when I came across you on the walkway? Why don't you start there for now?" Phillip suggested, sipping his wine and releasing his hold on her hand.

Susan sighed and figured she might just benefit from talking to Phillip. "You're sure you want to hear all of this? I haven't ever talked about it, so I can't guarantee it will make too much sense."

Phillip nodded, and Susan wished he would take her hand again, just for the connection that she had felt. It made her feel like she had a lifeline, something to prevent her from losing her way in the past.

Gazing back toward the fireplace, Susan took a sip of wine, and found the thread of the nightmarish path she would no longer keep at bay. "Well, you asked for it..." she whispered, and began to tell her story.

14

Susan came home from work the day after Taylor's tenth birthday. Joe sat at the kitchen table with three bold, white lines of cocaine spread before him. Silently, Susan walked into Taylor's room, where she found her children curled up in bed while *The Jungle Book* played. Rodney was asleep, and Susan watched him for a moment, enjoying the calm before the storm. She kissed them both without a word. Taylor's eyes never left Susan's face.

"You saw your father out there, honey?" Susan whispered. Taylor's large hazel eyes, mirrors of Susan's own, filled with tears as Taylor nodded yes.

"Taylor, I need you to stay in this room with your brother. No matter what happens, you do not open this door. Do you understand?" Taylor understood the seriousness of her mother's voice and directions. "I am locking the door behind me, sweetheart. I really need for you to do what I'm telling you, okay?"

Susan left the children's bedroom and walked into her own room. She packed up a suitcase with Joe's clothing and then made her way to the front door. Joe remained at the table, his eyes glazing over with the effects of the drugs that were no longer in lines on the tabletop. He looked over to where Susan had placed the suitcase and sneered.

"Going somewhere?" He laughed.

"No, but you are," Susan said, mustering up every bit of courage she could find. She walked over and took the phone off of the hook, as Joe's dazed expression followed her.

"I'm not going anywhere, bitch," Joe laughed.

"You are going. You are going to get up and leave this house and never come back. I'm all done Joe. You have broken promises to me for the last time. So, get out, or I will call the police and you will be arrested for possession and use of drugs," Susan said, shocked that she was able to sound so calm.

"Really? So, you're going to risk calling the police and having the kids see their own father get arrested? Is that what you're threatening me with, Susan?" Joe was stoned, and Susan knew he would have the false courage that came with his high.

Before Joe could get up, Susan dialed 9-1-1. Joe laughed, and Susan realized that he didn't believe she would do anything. Her years of living in fear and staying despite the abuse had given Joe the confidence to do whatever he wished.

Susan heard the operator answer, asking what the emergency was, and stood frozen in shame. She had allowed this to continue, and she was the only person who would be able to make it stop.

The operator asked again, and Susan finally answered. "Yes, my name is Susan Birge, at 385 Plains Way. My husband is under the influence of cocaine, and I am afraid for the lives of myself and my two young children," Susan explained. Still, Joe sat quietly, watching her as she spoke.

"Yes, I need the police here as soon as possible, please," Susan said to the operator.

Joe laughed out loud, and even offered, "Hey, don't forget to tell them about the stash in my toolbox out in the garage and the guns in the storage shed too."

Susan could hear the operator asking her questions. "Yes, that's my husband talking in the background. Yes, I'll stay on the line. Thank you, Carrie," Susan said into the phone.

"Whew girl, I've gotta give you credit this time around. You're doing a great job of weaving this one today," Joe said, as he stood to a staggering position. He walked over to the refrigerator and took out a cold beer. "You don't really think I believe you're calling the cops, do you?"

Susan never took her eyes off her husband. The operator kept telling Susan to leave, but Susan knew she would never leave her kids alone in the house with Joe again. She had thought about taking Rodney and Taylor over to Mrs. Arlen's before confronting Joe, but she didn't want them out of her sight. Joe could make his way there and once again use them as leverage. Even more, Joe could dispose of the drugs and other items before the police arrived, leaving Susan to handle the fallout afterward.

Susan knew this was her last chance to save her children. There was going to be no more backing down and giving in to Joe.

The operator was still talking to Susan, asking her again to leave the house. Susan hadn't said anything in a few minutes, and was beginning to worry how long it would take the police to arrive.

"Gee, Susan, give it up and hang up the phone already. We both know you're not going to do shit about the way I live, and you're certainly not going to be calling the cops on me." As he finished, Joe smashed his empty beer bottle on the edge of the sink, sending small shards of glass into the room. Susan felt a sting as one hit her cheek, but resisted the urge to wipe at it.

The operator was demanding a response and Susan knew she had to answer.

"Yes, Carrie, I'm still here. How much longer?" Susan asked, as Joe leered at her and walked her way.

"Oh, so is 'Carrie' still on the line, Susan? Why don't you let me talk to her then, sweetheart?" Joe was only a few feet away. Susan began to walk backward, trying not to take her eyes off of Joe as she felt a line of blood run down her cheek.

Carrie's voice was calmer now, and she was reassuring Susan that the police would be there any moment. She also kept telling Susan not to hang up or give the phone to Joe.

All of a sudden, sirens could be heard in the background. Just as Susan felt a surge of relief, she realized that Joe could also hear the approach of law enforcement.

"You bitch!" he screamed, lunging at the phone. Susan dodged, and ran toward the front door, hoping to lure Joe away from the children's room and toward the police. "I am going to kill you!" Joe promised, lunging at her again.

Susan made it to the front door, trying to pull it open and get outside. Joe slammed into her, smashing her into the wooden frame, and knocking the phone from her grasp. The wind was knocked out of her, and she fought against the panic that was engulfing her.

Joe was beyond reason, fueled by years of Susan's helplessness and by the courage of the drugs running freely in his bloodstream. Grabbing a handful of her hair, he smashed her head into the door. Susan screamed in pain, feeling blood run down her forehead and into her eyes. Out of the corner of her eye, she saw the flashing lights of at least one police cruiser and silently prayed that they would be able to stop her husband in time to save her children.

Unable to open the door, Susan tried to swing away from Joe, but he had a firm hold on her now. He flung her backward, and she tripped over the suitcase that she had filled earlier. She had been stupid to think she could reason with this crazy person. Even if he had been sane at some point, Susan knew that especially under the influence of the cocaine and alcohol, she had never stood a chance.

Still, she had made her stand, and so be it, she was not giving in this time. Susan rolled over onto her side trying to cover her head and felt Joe standing over her. She turned in time to see Joe pick up the heavy flower vase from the ledge by the front door. The police were out front, and Susan could hear them pounding on the front door, demanding to be let inside.

"Looks like they were just a bit too late, huh, wife?" Joe said as he raised the vase upward in order to gain momentum and smash it downward onto Susan's head.

As she felt the last moments of her life approaching, there was screaming from the hallway. Susan moved her eyes to see

Taylor standing there, yelling louder than Susan thought possible. Joe was distracted for just that small moment, giving Susan time to roll out of range as he let loose of the vase. It struck just inches away, directly where her head had been only seconds before, and Susan knew that Taylor had saved her life.

Joe looked down at her, and then the police were in the house, the shattered door agape behind them, and the wreckage of her family in front of them. Joe was restrained quickly and then Taylor was at Susan's side, her sobbing breaking Susan into tiny pieces. Finding the strength to wrap her arms around Taylor's fragile ten-year-old body took everything Susan had left. The police helped her to the couch and let her comfort her daughter.

That was when Susan remembered Rodney was still in the house. "Taylor! Where is your brother?" Susan cried out.

"I locked him in the bedroom, Mom," Taylor told her. "I knew I had to help you, but I didn't want Rodney to get hurt. So I covered him with the blanket and locked the door behind me when I came out here."

A nearby policeman heard the exchange. "You have someone else in the house, ma'am?" he asked Susan.

"Yes sir, my two-year-old son is in the bedroom there," Susan said pointing to the children's door. "It's locked though, so…" Susan's voice trailed off as she looked out of the front window and saw Joe in the back of a police cruiser. He was staring at her with clear rage. Susan felt fear run through her and began to shake uncontrollably.

The officer standing next to her whispered to a female officer and sent her down the hallway to get Rodney. He looked down at Susan after following her gaze to Joe. Moving his body in front of her to block Joe's line of vision, he gently placed his hand on Susan's shoulder.

"It's all over now, Mrs. Birge. He won't be able to hurt you again," he told Susan.

Susan's sob caught in her throat, and she hugged Taylor to her side. "Never again," Susan whispered softly. Then she looked at Taylor and said more strongly, "He will never hurt us again."

Rodney was carried out of the bedroom, having slept through the entire drama. The female officer placed him in Susan's lap, still wrapped in the blanket with which Taylor had thought to cover him. Susan sat quietly on the couch, both of her children safe in her arms, and rocked them gently.

Susan was looked over by the medical team that arrived, and once the officers felt the situation was under control, Susan and the kids were escorted to the local police station. Statements were taken, and Susan felt exhaustion wash over her. But, the children were treated like royalty, served donuts and hot chocolate, and given soft stuffed animals to hold onto while Susan told the police everything. She wanted to be sure that Joe never got to them again, and she was smart enough to know how hard it was to convict domestic abusers.

• • •

To say that Joe didn't take the ending of the marriage well would be the understatement of the century. Immediately after Joe's arrest Susan filed for divorce along with personal protection orders that she received for her and the children. The court provided counselors for all of them, and Susan became surer of her decision each and every day. She learned more about the cycle of abuse, and vowed that never again would she place her well being in the hands of anyone other than herself.

Since the evidence was so strong against his client, Joe's court-appointed attorney convinced him to accept a plea bargain. Along with the tape-recorded emergency 9-1-1 call, there were also the many police eyewitnesses to the scene in the house that dreadful day. Sweet Mrs. Arlen from next door had come forward and given a powerful statement as well, avowing to the abuse of Susan and the marks and bruises she had witnessed over the years.

Joe was sentenced to three to five years with the chance of parole based on good behavior. He was not allowed to contact Susan or the children, either on his own or through outside contacts. While Joe was in prison, Susan's divorce was finalized, moving quickly through the process with the help of the arresting officers and other witnesses and counselors who all spoke on behalf of Susan and Taylor's ordeal.

Rodney, who was so young, seemed oblivious to everything that was happening. Occasionally he would ask where his daddy was, but Taylor became an expert at steering his questions away from Susan. The counselors warned Susan that she needed to watch for problems later, but for now they had done what they could to help with the transition.

Less than a year after she was almost killed, Susan took her children and left the town where she had spent most of her married years to Joe. Not wanting to have a different last name from her children, she decided to keep Birge. She had been working at a local flower shop, using her natural talents to create beautiful things for other people. With the money she had saved, she knew she needed to get away. If he made early parole Joe could have been released in as little as eighteen months. Susan wanted to be gone without leaving a trail. Though Joe had sworn he wanted nothing else to do with them, Susan wanted to put space between them so she'd never run into him again. She knew better than to trust Joe would stay away.

So, she packed up their belongings, loaded up the rather dilapidated used car she bought, and headed away from Chicago. Originally, Susan didn't know where she would go. She looked through atlases and maps, but in the end decided to simply drive east. She was ready for a quiet place, with quiet people, to safely raise her children.

While she sat at a breakfast diner a few days into the trip, Susan happened to see a commercial on television. She asked the waitress about the scene before her, and that was when she had decided upon Connecticut. It was far away from home, and seemed like a completely new and better world.

• • •

"...and a lifetime from then, here I am," Susan finished, looking at Phillip. He had kept his word and not interrupted her once with questions or accusations. Susan noticed that the wine bottle was almost empty and held up her goblet in question.

"I promised not to judge and to fill your glass," Phillip laughed. "I always keep my word."

"Well, thank you. Thank you for listening and for refilling," she added. "So, now what? You know the ugly truth, so should I look away and give you a chance to run away like you're on fire? Do you want to fake your pager going off so you have a gentlemanly reason to go?"

Phillip looked around the room, lit now with the dusky light from the large windows and the glow of the fireplace. He waved his hand to the waiter, and Susan knew a beautiful thing was coming to an end. She'd never told this story to anyone in her new life, and now she had ruined a budding friendship.

The waiter moved promptly to the table, having kept his word not to interfere in the interim. "Yes, sir?"

"We'd like to see menus now please, if it's okay with you?" he said, inclining his head toward Susan.

Susan nodded, shocked, and looked down at the napkin in her lap. It was a very fancy napkin, she noticed. She tried to distract her body from the need to sob in relief. Even though it had been almost fifteen years ago, the past had a way of not letting go. Telling her story had released a weight from her that she hadn't realized she was carrying.

Phillip was kind enough not to push. He could see that her nerves were raw with the telling of the horror she had lived through in her former life. So, the new friends sat quietly, enjoying the ambience and delicious meal, along with each other's presence. After indulging in a decadent chocolate dessert, he followed her safely home, waving good-bye as she pulled into her driveway shortly before she expected Rodney to return.

Susan could only hope that the fresh start she felt beginning would also belong to her son. Rodney needed a good omen, and Susan prayed this was it for her son as well.

She walked inside the house determined to call Taylor. It had been too long since they had all been together as a family. It was time to correct that mistake too. If only she felt Rodney agreed.

15

Rodney woke up early the next morning, unable to sleep as nervousness ran through his body. He had dreamed that he had gone to school to find he'd been placed into all special education classes. His mind was blank, he could remember nothing, and every person in the school knew he was a huge loser.

"Great way to start," he muttered to himself, dragging his sore body out of bed and into the bathroom. A long, scalding hot shower was just what he needed. Every muscle in his body ached from the hours of hard basketball he'd played the afternoon before at OYC. The guys there showed no mercy, and Rodney was developing powerful skills as he played against the strength of the street players. He had even hit a few three-point shots in the last game, earning himself chest bumps and high fives from his teammates, as well as good-natured insults from the other team.

Rodney had walked home on high energy, and even managed to be cordial to his mom. Mr. Oakes's comments were still fresh in Rodney's head, and he had decided to give this a shot. Maybe he had been wrong. Maybe his mom was doing everything she knew how to help him.

The hot water ran down his body, and Rodney sighed in relief. He could feel his muscles loosening under the onslaught of the massaging showerhead. Trying to ignore the knot of fear in his belly, Rodney lathered with his favorite shower gel. His mother must have bought it for him as a surprise.

Rodney smiled as he remembered how his mom used to make him smiley-face pancakes on his first days of school. Even when he told her that he was too old for such baby stuff, she had only smiled and poured the syrup onto the stack of love. This year he had been such a mess that he hadn't even eaten them. Instead, he had scowled at her and made a cruel comment before heading outside to meet his friends. Rodney remembered how he had gone so far as to mock his mom to the group and turned to laugh as she stood in the kitchen window watching him leave for his junior year of high school.

Despite how horrible he had been in the past, though, his mom was always there to help him when he needed it. Mr. Oakes had been trying to get that idea into Rodney's thick head and had finally cracked the noggin a bit. Maybe this time would be different.

Heading downstairs a bit later, smelling great and feeling better, Rodney and his damp hair moved into the kitchen to see his mother standing at the pancake griddle.

Susan turned around as she heard Rodney. She swiveled to the table, a full plate of smiley-face pancakes in her hand, and laid it down with a flourish at Rodney's seat.

"Breakfast is served," she said in her best English accent.

Rodney just stood there and out of nowhere felt his eyes tear up. He felt so stupid. He was sixteen, and he was going to cry about pancakes. His mom quickly began to apologize.

"Rodney, I'm sorry. I know you're too old for these, but I just thought, this is kind of like a first day of school, and…" Susan's voice trailed off, and she reached for the plate as if to dispose of the evidence.

"Mom!" Rodney yelled, wiping his face roughly with the back of his hand. "No, this is great, it's just…"

Susan stopped in her tracks, watching the battle play on her son's face. Without another word, she reached out and picked up the syrup, squeezing an ample amount onto the steaming stack. Rodney watched his mom pour and then walk over and take his hand.

"Come and eat, honey. You have a big day ahead of you," he heard her say softly. Rodney let his mom push him into his chair and then proceeded to eat every pancake she put in front of him. Maybe today would be as horrible as his nightmare, but right now, he was going to enjoy the simple act of eating smiley-face pancakes.

• • •

Less than an hour later, Rodney stood outside the front of Oxford High School, its imposing brick façade screaming that Rodney did not belong. He knew that his mom hadn't had an easy time of leaving him here, but Rodney had assured her he was fine. They both knew he was lying through his teeth, but for once his mom let him get away with it, not pushing for more. After giving her a shaky smile of reassurance, he had pushed open the door and stepped out onto the sidewalk, knocking on the roof of the car to let her know to drive away.

Rodney knew it was now or never and with a strong cleansing breath took the first step toward the building. He had arrived about twenty minutes earlier than usual, so he wasn't surrounded by hundreds of other students. Five steps up to the landing, another five to the front doors, and then without letting himself think about it Rodney entered the school.

It still smelled the same he realized with a start. He made his way down the hallway to his math class and looked inside to see Miss Bell. She had always been his favorite teacher in high school. She had never gone easy on him and had let him know that she expected greatness from him. It had made him laugh at first, and he had pushed her buttons, hoping to get her to back off and leave him alone. That hadn't worked out, but in the end it had been the best thing for him, as Miss Bell had known.

While many teachers simply let Rodney slough off his assignments and treated him like he knew nothing, Miss Bell called on Rodney in class for answers. She even let him illustrate different solutions on the smart board the district had installed the year before to help with student achievement. She made sure he did the work and actually turned it in, never accepting zeros. It had been a hell of a shock to him in the beginning! Rodney had never been so glad that his school day started with math as he was today.

Clearing his throat, he walked farther into the room, startling the young woman. When Miss Bell saw that it was Rodney, her face instantly broke into a smile, and she moved back to greet him.

"Rodney! I'm so glad you're back in school where you belong," she said with obvious sincerity.

Rodney dropped his head so his bangs covered his expression. With a noncommittal grunt, he handed the large stack of make-up work to her and waited. With the help of Veronica at OYC, Rodney had been able to get completely caught up with his work and felt pretty confident about not being totally lost.

Miss Bell leafed through the stack exclaiming, "Rodney, this is amazing! I never thought you would get all this work finished so quickly. Do you need any help? Have any questions?"

"Nah, or, not about math anyway," Rodney admitted.

Giving him time, Miss Bell remained quiet, sitting on top of a desk and gesturing for Rodney to do the same.

"Any idea on how I'm supposed to get through this day without losing it?" Rodney asked humorously, but knowing for him it was a completely serious topic. It had been so nice falling into a routine at OYC. Being back at his old stomping grounds was scaring the hell out of him, and he felt like he was standing on the verge of a bottomless chasm. One wrong step would send him falling, never to be seen or heard from again. Now that he'd seen a glimpse of light he was going to do his best at avoiding that fatal footfall.

Miss Bell hadn't said anything, and after a few moments Rodney looked up from underneath his wall of bangs to see her watching him and smiling.

"Oh, Rodney, you'll know what to do if you just trust yourself. I have great faith in you, young man. You're not my favorite for nothing, you know!" Miss Bell added with a laugh. It was a running classroom joke among Miss Bell's students that she told at least forty kids a day they were her favorite, sharing the honor equally among her students throughout the year.

Giving in to the need to release the pressure building in his chest, Rodney let loose of the laugh inside of him, smiling at his teacher.

"Yeah, I always knew I was your fave," he said. "I mean, really… could there be any competition with a face like this?" At this, Rodney contorted his face into the most ridiculous caricature he could fathom.

Miss Bell got off the desk and leaned over to tousle Rodney's hair into a mess. "I have missed you, Mr. Birge," she said as she moved back to the front of the class. "Now, are you going to hide in here until first bell, or are you ready to face kids in the hallways?" she asked seriously.

"Well, if it's all the same to you, I think I'll just sit here and hide. I mean," Rodney started in his very best deeply mature voice, "I would greatly benefit from absorbing the mathematical knowledge of your teaching environment ma'am."

"You are always welcome in my class, Rodney," Miss Bell said to him. "No matter what happens, I believe in you. You come to me when you need help today. You hear me?" she added, sharing her smile with the students who were beginning to show up for first period.

Rodney opened up his bag. He had put every single necessary item for his day inside of it that morning so he didn't have to visit his locker and meet the goons he knew would be awaiting his return. There hadn't been a single contact from Melinda or

Alan since his arrest, but Rodney knew Melinda wouldn't just let him off her radar so easily.

Taking out his math text, a pencil, and a clean sheet of paper, he smiled at Miss Bell and nodded. However, Rodney knew this day was going to be far from smooth.

16

L eaving her only son standing outside the school that morning had been a new addition to the "hardest things she'd ever done" list. Susan knew Rodney had tried to put on a great face, acting the clown a bit to ease her mind; but she had sensed the tension in his body and wanted to hug him and keep him with her to protect him from all the temptations that awaited him inside.

School was supposed to be a safe place, but she knew that it didn't work like that these days for many youngsters. Schools were rampant with drugs and alcohol and gang influences. Many teachers felt that kids like Rodney didn't deserve another chance and were a waste of their time. Susan could only pray that Rodney would last out this first day, probably his hardest on this new track.

"One day at a time," she whispered aloud as she unlocked the florist shop and went inside to the smell of already brewing coffee. She had learned years ago that presetting the timer gave her a better chance of being awake and energetic. Now the rich, earthy aroma of Columbia's finest beans greeted her. Today was certain to be a two-potter, and she wasn't ashamed to admit to this tiny addiction.

As she was putting her purse away in her office cabinet, Susan heard the bells signaling the door's opening. It wasn't unusual for her to have a customer as soon as she opened. She definitely needed a distraction from the image of Rodney's back disappearing into the building that housed the negative influences he'd lost contact with the past two weeks.

Putting on her best customer service expression, Susan walked up front to see whose life she could improve with floral magic. Phillip was standing in front of the counter, holding out a large coffee from the local patisserie. She couldn't help but smile at him as she saw him standing in her small, cozy shop in his uniform.

"I thought I could start your day off with a fresh java, but I can smell you've already gone there today." Phillip laughed as she took the cup.

"There will not be enough coffee for me today," Susan said, sipping appreciatively with closed eyes and a deep intake of air. "Nothing smells better than hot coffee in the morning," she said smiling up at him

"So, how did it go this morning? Did Rodney seem to be handling the back-to-school routine?" Phillip asked, not wasting much time in getting to his subject.

Susan couldn't help being a bit disappointed, hoping for a moment that perhaps Phillip had come in just to see her. She had learned from her past, however, not to count on someone else for her happiness, and promised herself to take Phillip's presence at face value.

"It was as good as I could have expected," Susan said. She filled Phillip in on how she had made the pancakes and how nervous both she and Rodney had been as they drove to the school.

"Actually," Phillip said, moving around the shop and touching a display here and there, "the fact that Rodney seemed edgy is probably a good sign. Most kids return to their pre-offense cockiness and jump right back in with their crowd. That's what leads them down the same path and back into the court system. The fact that Rodney's tether didn't alert while on his suspension is amazing, Susan." He glimpsed her worried expression.

Phillip hadn't really needed to check in with Susan, but he couldn't seem to stay away from her. All he could think of was the hell she had been through to make it to where she now stood. Susan Birge was an amazing woman, and he hadn't felt drawn to someone like this in quite a long time.

Susan was pleased to hear the positive feedback from Phillip. After all, he was part of the system and seemed like the kind of person who would not sugarcoat the truth.

"So," she asked Phillip, "do you mind if I ask how the arrangement went over with its recipient?" As soon as the words were out of her mouth, Susan wanted to scoop them back again. Her words seemed so obvious, as if she were trying to dig out his relationship status.

"Recipient?" Phillip asked. "Well, I for one loved it, and it actually lasted quite a bit longer than I had expected. My roommate seemed less appreciative though."

"She doesn't like flowers?" Susan asked casually, keeping the pang of disappointment from her voice.

"Well, I think it's just hard for a basset hound to appreciate much of anything aside from belly rubs and chewy treats," Phillip explained, laughing. "My dog, Tubs, is a total slug!"

Susan couldn't help but laugh at herself and at the image that jumped into her head of a portly dog with big sleepy eyes and Phillip lying on the couch scratching its belly. For some reason she caught a fit of the giggles and gave in to it, allowing herself to laugh out loud. Her tension released.

"Phillip, I'm sorry!" Susan said, holding the counter and wiping her eyes. "Tubs?" she said, trying to fight down another round of laughter.

Phillip was enjoying this, Susan's eyes sparkling with enjoyment. For a moment he let his mind wander to the ways he could add enjoyment to her life and then chastised himself for letting his business life clash with more personal ideas. Susan had been through too much, and his attentions might be seen as interference. He enjoyed spending time with Susan and didn't want to jeopardize their new friendship.

As Susan finished laughing, she looked up to see Phillip gazing at her, and though she dismissed it immediately, she thought she had seen a spark that had nothing to do with Rodney or Tubs. She felt herself stand a bit taller and was glad that she had taken the time to add some makeup to her routine today. The woman in her had been pushed down for years, but there were moments when she reveled in a man's attentions.

Rather than ignore it, Susan let her instincts run with the desire to flirt a bit with the man standing in front of her in her otherwise deserted floral shop. Leaning in just a bit, Susan looked at Phillip, giving him the full power of her hazel-brown eyes.

"So, your only roommate is Tubs? Or, is there someone special of a human sort that you live with, Officer Reynolds?" Susan said softly, tipping her head down just a bit to let her bangs mysteriously shield her eyes.

Phillip felt a jolt through his body and fought the sudden urge to kiss Susan. His right hand clutched the countertop to keep his body in place. It took a willpower that he wasn't sure he really wanted to contain, but knew he should at the moment.

Susan was flirting with him, perhaps dangerously. She knew suddenly from his reaction that Phillip had responded to her question. Not since she had fled to Oxford with her children had she given an opening to anyone. Now, she acknowledged, her body was feeling the void.

Phillip resisted the need to lean into Susan, but also didn't lean away as he probably should if he was going to maintain a professional stance. "Just me and Tubs," he said to Susan, letting his eyes wander over her face.

"What a shame that the flowers went to waste," Susan added, remaining inches from Phillip now.

With a deep rumble of a chuckle from his chest, Phillip moved slightly closer to Susan. "Trust me, they were greatly appreciated.

Every single time I looked at them, I thought about you standing in the back of your shop. I thought about the way your hands had chosen each stem and the love that went into the placing of the different flowers. I thought about the way you touched them and wondered at the passion you put into the arrangement, seemingly without conscious thought."

Susan was afraid to move. She had gone down this forgotten path and now wasn't quite sure which way to continue. There hadn't been a man in her life since Joe. She had never had a desire to fill that space and instead had filled her life with her children and her flowers. She could feel her blood throbbing beneath her skin.

The bells above the door jingled softly, and both Susan and Phillip automatically stepped back. Susan could feel the flush of her skin, and even as she acknowledged the disappointment of unknown fulfillment, she was secretly relieved that she had been saved from making the next move.

Smiling at the lifesaving customer, Susan smoothed her apron and moved to do her job. Phillip stayed where he was, and as Susan brushed past him to help the man who had entered the store, she heard a rattled breath escape his chest. Susan grinned, reassured that it had not been a misunderstanding on her part. She had worked her feminine skills, and though they were dusty from sitting on the shelf unused so many years, they were still in decent working order. Her skin flushed and her eyes sparkled.

The customer at the counter seemed quite taken with Susan's sparkle too. He had come in to choose a birthday bouquet for his mother, and as he talked the man moved, blocking Susan from Phillip's line of sight. He drew Susan into conversation about different flowers, asking about her favorites. Susan smiled politely as the customer complimented her eyes and her smile.

As she graciously waved off this unexpected attention, Susan remained aware of Phillip's presence. She was distracted, wondering if they might pick up where they had left off once her customer was finished with his purchase. As she gathered flowers for the birthday bouquet, she allowed herself to imagine what it might be like to kiss Phillip. His radio went off and Susan realized that Phillip was leaving.

"Ms. Birge," Phillip said, stepping up and subtly putting his body between Susan and the other man. "I'll see you soon to continue our conversation if that's all right with you?"

Susan couldn't think straight, as the two men seemed to vie for her attention. So, instead of words, Susan looked at Phillip, her need clear upon her face, as she nodded at him and moved behind the counter to help her customer.

Phillip seemed to sense her struggle and smiled as he turned to get back to work. Susan watched him leave, concerned all of a sudden about the dangers of Phillip's profession.

Phillip turned back to catch her eye from the sidewalk just as the flirting customer leaned over the counter to say something to Susan. Susan turned, giving her full attention to the customer and the flowers she was wrapping. Perhaps Phillip needed a bit of motivation to get back to her sooner rather than later, Susan thought.

It was going to be a great day, she vowed, sending positive thoughts toward her son as well. Though it was her son's decision to stay on track or not, a little positive thinking from his mom couldn't hurt. She knew Rodney was going to need all the help he could get.

17

Rodney had made it through the first three classes of his day. Miss Bell had given him the start he needed, and Rodney had avoided his locker and the crowd that hung out in that hallway area. He still hadn't seen his group of friends, and Rodney was hoping this luck could hold out all day. Even though his history and computer teachers hadn't given him any grief, they hadn't exactly been showing him the love that Miss Bell had either.

Rodney wasn't stupid. He knew that most of the kids and staff were aware of why he'd been suspended for ten days. He also knew that many people could care less at this point whether Rodney stayed out of trouble or simply disappeared.

Lunch was posing a problem for Rodney, and he wasn't sure how to handle the cafeteria. If he showed up there Melinda and Alan would expect him to hang with them. Rodney also knew the judge had been clear that he should stay away from the group he'd been in so much trouble with before appearing in court the last time.

It was odd to Rodney that he hadn't seen his buddy, Alan, yet. Of course, Rodney was pretty sure that Alan feared retribution for leaving the car that afternoon in the parking lot. If Alan had stayed, they both would have been busted and taken in, but the unwritten rule was that you didn't bail on your friends. Rodney shook his head as he remembered how stupid he'd been, staying in the car and taunting the school security guard. If he'd run like Alan, he wouldn't have ended up in jail.

Of course, if he hadn't been arrested, he wouldn't have met Veronica and the other kids at Oxford Youth Center or Mr. Oakes. He wouldn't be able to say that he'd been clean for two solid weeks. Honestly, Rodney was surprised by how little he missed getting high. Filling his life with the center's activities, basketball, and getting his grades up to standard had been a great boost to his morale. Rodney was actually starting to believe that this time could be better.

Another big plus had been the relationship with his mom. It had been a long time since Rodney had felt like his mom wanted to spend time with him. Though, in all fairness, he also knew that it was mostly his own fault. Rodney knew he hadn't been the best kid, but sometimes he just felt so pissed off that he didn't know how to stop the rage that overtook him.

Suddenly, Rodney got jostled into the stand of lockers he was walking past. He felt his elbow jab into the lock, and reacting to the pain he spun around to yell at the culprit. "What's your problem, dude?" he yelled as he turned around and looked into the shocked, round eyes of Veronica.

Rodney was speechless. He could only stand there, watching Veronica, rubbing the soreness from his sure-to-be-bruised elbow.

"Oh my gosh, Rodney, I am so sorry!" Veronica said, leaning around to look at his arm. "Are you all right?" she added, reaching out to rub his elbow.

Rodney felt like he had died and gone to Heaven. "I am now," he said, laughing as Veronica gave him the "shut up" look he had come to recognize.

"Idiot," she muttered, and they both laughed. Veronica had used the word so many times during their tutoring sessions at OYC that Rodney had teasingly decided it was Veronica's pet name for him.

"Why didn't you tell me you went to my school?" Rodney asked, still surprised to find her friendly face in the hallway.

"Guess you never asked, huh?" Veronica answered with a grin.

"Guess my slave-driver tutor never gave me much chance," Rodney answered with a grin of his own.

The first lunch bell rang, and Rodney's stomach rumbled in protest. Veronica laughed and nodded her head toward the cafeteria. "Heading to lunch?" She smiled.

"Yeah, though, to be honest..." he said sheepishly, "I'm not so sure how to handle it today." *What the hell is wrong with me,* he thought. He knew better than to show signs of weakness, especially with a girl he desperately wanted to impress.

Veronica was standing very still in front of him. Rather than being disgusted by his honest expression of fear, though, she seemed impressed. "Has it been horrible, having to come back and deal with all of this again?" she asked.

"Hasn't been too bad so far," he admitted, before making the decision to continue on his honesty path. "Not sure how I'm going to avoid my old friends at lunch though," he told her, swallowing his pride and throwing the information out into the open.

Veronica's forehead scrunched in confusion. "Didn't you hear?" she asked Rodney. Then she realized that he had been out of the information loop for a couple of weeks and probably hadn't heard any recent news. When Rodney shook his head in response, Veronica explained. "There was a big drug bust last week. Cops came in with the search dogs, lockers were all opened up while the kids were kept in the cafeterias, and there were like fifteen students who got busted. Most of them got suspended, but a few even made it to the possible expulsion list."

Rodney suddenly knew why he hadn't heard from Melinda or Alan while he was gone. First, it made sense that Alan had been avoiding Rodney's possible anger after being left hanging. If Alan had been busted himself there was no way he would have gotten in touch with Rodney. Though Rodney got irritated with his mom's interference, he also knew that her intervention had given him extra chances to stay out of trouble. Melinda was in a foster home, but basically did what she wanted. Alan didn't have

parents who cared enough to help him. He'd basically been living on his own since fifth grade, so if he was busted it would be
that much harder for Alan to get back on track.

"Damn, I didn't know anything about it, Veronica," Rodney
admitted, as his mind swept past the guilt he was feeling at
the relief of not having to see the crew in the lunchroom and
hallways.

"Yeah, it was a pretty bad scene," Veronica said. She knew
Rodney was probably glad not to have the pressure. Still, he and
Alan had been friends based on what Rodney had shared with
her during the tutoring sessions.

Looking back at Veronica, Rodney crooked his elbow and
turned toward the cafeteria. "Might I escort you to lunch?" he
gallantly offered.

Veronica laughed in a friendly sort of way, swatting his arm
away as she did so. "Come on, clown," she said, dragging him
down the hallway. Neither of them saw the slouched figure standing at the other end of the lockers, watching them with anger
and pure hatred on her face.

18

Without the worry of running into his old crew, Rodney was able to actually enjoy his lunch with Veronica. They ended up sharing a pizza basket, which consisted of three slices of greasy pepperoni and a bin of French fries. Veronica teased him about scarfing down most of the fries with more ketchup than was legal in Connecticut. Rodney used to skip eating lunch for the more lackadaisical slouching at a back table with his group before they'd go outside to have a smoke off campus. Often they would then skip their next class. If Rodney did make it to his physical education class after lunch, he was usually too hungry and tired to participate in any positive way. More often than not, Mr. Kruse would simply ignore Rodney, or if he were in a particularly foul mood he would send him to the office for the hour.

Today, Rodney walked out of the cafeteria feeling pretty good about things in general. He waved good-bye to Veronica as she made a left down the hallway to her advanced-placement history class. Rodney actually made it to the gym with time to spare. Mr. Kruse did a double take as he saw Rodney dressed and ready to go, seated in his squad for the class assignment.

"Well, Mr. Birge, so glad that you could join us here today," Mr. Kruse said as he stood before the rows of students to take roll call.

"Me too," Rodney smiled back at the burly former football player turned coach and teacher. Rodney's sincerely happy answer made the man laugh and shake his head.

"I will never understand you kids," Rodney heard him mutter as he continued down the row.

As if the fates had aligned and decided that Rodney should have a spectacular first day back to school, Mr. Kruse announced that for the next two weeks they would be playing basketball. Rodney couldn't keep the grin from his face as Mr. Kruse began to cover the basics, emphasizing that for the first few days they would be focusing on learning the proper techniques of the game and then they would be in teams for three-on-three tournament style eliminations.

"The winning team of the tournament will be awarded an extraordinary prize, much sought after by all," Mr. Kruse said loudly. The class erupted in groans of disbelief as Mr. Kruse held up what had to be the gaudiest trophy ever created. It stood only a foot tall, but was topped by a large, bedazzled basketball. The ball sat nestled in a gold and silver basketball hoop, and as Rodney watched, the net of the hoop began to twinkle with multiple colored lights.

Fifty students roared in appreciation as Mr. Kruse took a dramatic bow. "Now, I know how badly you all want this for your fireplace mantles at home, but that doesn't mean you will be allowed to get away with any poor sportsmanship or illegal basketball tricks. We'll be playing standard rules not street ball, so keep that in mind."

Students were whispering to each other, nudging and pointing at the trophy. *Mr. Kruse knows how to get us motivated,* Rodney thought, as the team members started to gather together. It had been so long since he had actually cared about anything at school. He was caught off guard when he realized he was thinking about his mother's expression if he were to come home with the trophy in tow. He couldn't remember the last time he had been able to show her something from school that didn't involve detentions, failing report cards, or notices of school-board hearings.

As Rodney heard his name called and went to join his team, he decided that the glowing basketball hoop was perfect to begin earning a new reputation both at home and at school.

• • •

His final hour of the day was fifth-period English with Mrs. Rule. Even before Rodney had started to struggle in her class, Mrs. Rule had made it clear she didn't appreciate his presence in her sacred room. Rodney had always done fairly well in English classes, or he would have had he bothered to turn in his assignments. He had been reading since he was about four years old, having found a way to escape from sadness into the world of make-believe. When he had first come home from school, his heart breaking over his father's absence in his life, it had been the world of Narnia that had rescued him. His mother would read aloud to him, until finally Rodney realized he could decode the letters and words into the stories they held all on his own.

Words had always come easy on paper for Rodney, but if he found it easy to disappear into the stories, it was sometimes just as difficult to connect with the teacher and classroom expectations. Rodney always sat in the back of the rooms, waiting to see for himself what the teacher would be like. He had learned pretty quickly that it was safest for him to judge people as harshly as they judged him.

• • •

On the first day of school that year, Rodney entered Mrs. Rule's room, went to the back as usual, and slumped down to wait. Mrs. Rule was definitely old school and Rodney knew by the look on her face that she wasn't going to have an open mind about him. Sure enough, Mrs. Rule's first move was to have each student share the last book they had read. The honor student beside Rodney finished sharing about the vampire trilogy she had completed over the summer. "Lovely, Miss Holloway. Thank you."

Then, Mrs. Rule turned toward Rodney. "And you?" she said, her sarcastic smile beaming.

Rodney battled between ignoring the woman, charging out of class, or putting on a great impression of Vinnie Barbarino, the dumbest boy in Mr. Kotter's class that he had watched on reruns for years. Instead, he took another route, anticipating the look of surprise on the old bat's face.

"Let me see, Mrs. Rule," Rodney started, putting on a pretentious manner. "I do believe the most recent book I read was Harper Lee's, *To Kill a Mockingbird*. Yes, yes, that's it. A most wonderful tale set in our country's embarrassing days of extreme bigotry and cultural chasms."

Rodney saw the shock move across Mrs. Rule's face, and then he waited. He knew what would be coming next, and Mrs. Rule did not let him down. Her surprise mutated into disbelief and then into the sureness of upcoming student humiliation.

"Truly, Mr. Birge?" Mrs. Rule went on the attack, glancing down at the student roster to use his name instead of other names Rodney was sure were running through her mind. "And what, pray tell, did you find most captivating in the classic literature of Harper Lee's story?" Rodney wasn't surprised. This was the usual path. First the teacher was shocked and then felt the inexplicable need to grind whatever bit of self-esteem the student might have left deep into the ground. This had always confused him. Teachers were supposed to want to inspire students to do their best jobs, and yet there were so many whose paths he had crossed that truly used all their powers to humiliate and degrade.

With a sigh, Rodney slouched back in his desk and gave Mrs. Rule a look of true disgust. "Quite what I thought," she said, turning her back to Rodney in dismissal.

Rodney let her take a few prim steps away from his desk, and then finished his answer. "It's difficult for me to pinpoint which part of Lee's plot I find most captivating, Mrs. Rule. However, I am able to articulate that one of my most powerful memories comes during the courtroom scenes. I believe I can relate so well with that section because of the unjustness of society toward the innocent defendant. For some reason, I can feel Jim's pain at being so harshly misunderstood. I can relate to how it must have felt for him to sit and listen to people wrongly accuse him. I can empathize with a man whose only guilt is his physical appearance, and the betrayal he must have felt as even those who knew him to be innocent jumped on the bandwagon of stereotyping and didn't even stick up for him or give him a chance to prove his worth."

Mrs. Rule froze in her steps as Rodney started to speak. She never turned all the way around to face him, but did give in and twist her head around as his tirade was so eloquently expressed in the room full of stunned students. When Rodney finished, his voice never louder than what would be acceptable in a classroom conversation, Mrs. Rule turned her head back around and without a word finished walking up to the front of the room.

"Bravo, dude," Rodney heard from a few rows over. Mrs. Rule turned her harsh look away from Rodney and set her anger to the new speaker.

"That will be enough!" she screeched, and the culprit, a red-eyed, spiky haired, probably also misunderstood student answered Mrs. Rule with a big smile and a thumbs-up sign.

After that, Rodney knew he had Mrs. Rule's number. It wouldn't matter what he did in her class, she would never give him a chance. To save them both the time and embarrassment, Rodney didn't bother to turn in the research papers and multiple page essays on the literature they read in class. He did the reading, allowing himself to savor the stories and exchange his existence for the characters' lives for a few hours here and there. Even though he had the intelligence, what Rodney lacked was the desire to play the games he felt were necessary to thrive in the world of Mrs. Rule and others like her. Rodney just didn't care to fight that battle.

• • •

So, now Rodney was back from his mandatory suspension. The first four hours of his day had been better than passable. Rodney had actually enjoyed himself, had the pleasure of eating lunch with Veronica, and hadn't had to deal with the crew at all. All he had to do was survive Mrs. Rule's final period and then he could head over to Oxford Youth Center and play janitor, get his homework done, and maybe shoot some hoops with the guys.

As soon as Rodney walked into the class, he knew something was wrong. Mrs. Rule was standing stiffly at the corner of her desk, obviously waiting for Rodney to show up in her room. Without saying a word, Mrs. Rule pointed to the desk directly in front of hers, where she sat each day without moving too much. She knew her literature, but Rodney could tell that she was a worn-out teacher ready to retire. Many of her assignments were straight out of the eighties, and Rodney was sure she had no idea of how to set up a blog or use the great Internet resources that could have made her class so much better for all of them.

"Here," she said to Rodney. "This is your new seat, Mr. Birge. I won't have you disrupting my class with your…issues."

Rodney swallowed the desire to hurl his backpack at the old woman's head and instead gently placed his bag on the desktop and sat down, primly folding his hands together and smiling sweetly up at Mrs. Rule's scowling face. Mrs. Rule had obviously not expected Rodney to comply, and this irritated him more than anything else so far. She had totally been setting him up he realized. Rage filled Rodney so fast that it nearly threw him from the front row desk. He ripped into his bag and pulled out a folder and a new pencil. His mother had filled his binder with new mechanical pencils, the ones she knew he preferred because of the sleekness of the writing utensil.

Seeing Mrs. Rule watching him carefully, Rodney suddenly realized that the old woman was terrified of him. He had never been disrespectful in her room, even though he hadn't turned in his work. Based on the stories that had probably been circulating through school, Mrs. Rule had judged and found Rodney guilty. *How am I supposed to change my life if this is going to be how people treat me?*

Rodney barely heard the bell ring. He watched Mrs. Rule move from her desk to the overhead table. She flipped on the old, dated projector and began to read the overhead screen information. Apparently the class had finished reading the classic Shakespeare irony, *Romeo and Juliet*, while he had been gone. Mrs. Rule was going over the project options and listing all of the necessary work that would be due over the next two weeks.

A stack of packets was placed on his desk, and Rodney passed them back without looking up at the teacher as she skittered past him. Rodney realized that Mrs. Rule hadn't counted on him actually sitting directly in front of her desk. She had probably thought Rodney would stomp out in a rage. Then, she could have followed through with more discipline, and this desk would have remained empty. Now, Rodney was in her direct line of vision, and she would be forced to see him each and every day he showed up in class.

With a renewed interest in the world of irony, Rodney began to leaf through the packet of questions, project ideas, and due dates that sat before him. Looking up a few minutes later, he saw Mrs. Rule looking at him nervously. Fighting the urge to scowl at her, or to pretend to jump at her, Rodney decided to kill her with kindness, and gave the biggest smile performed in his school day. Mrs. Rule looked quickly away, and Rodney could see the gulp of fear move down her throat.

Finally, Rodney thought, *this class is going to be interesting.* As students began working on the question packets, Rodney turned to the honor roll student, the vampire reader, and asked about what he had missed while he'd been on vacation. Vampire girl smiled at Rodney's humor, but true to her character, filled him in completely on the work. When the final bell rang, Rodney packed up and made his way out. Before closing the door behind him, however, he turned to Mrs. Rule who sat at her desk gazing out of the row of windows lost in thought.

"Thanks for the awesome welcome back, Mrs. Rule," Rodney said. "It's so nice to know that there are teachers who care so much about the welfare of students they've been entrusted with teaching." His voice was angelic, but the verbal irony was not lost on Mrs. Rule, who simply turned back to the windows as Rodney left. Rodney moved into the wave of students rushing outside to meet school busses and friends. First day down, he thought, starting his short walk to OYC. It was going to be a harder struggle than he'd imagined, but so far for very different reasons.

19

It had been almost a week since Phillip had been in the shop, and Susan was finding herself doubting her previous flirting. She was kicking herself for ruining what could have been an interesting friendship. As soon as that thought was out of her head though, she would find herself daydreaming about the actual event and the warmth that had flooded her that day in her shop.

Well then, where the hell has he been since Monday? She asked herself repeatedly. Maybe he had lied about having someone special in his life. More than likely, after he had left, Phillip had reviewed what a mess Susan's life was as well as the many reasons he should run away. She couldn't blame him for that at least. If the situation was reversed, Susan wouldn't go anywhere near him.

Susan realized that her frazzled state of mind was not helping the flowers that waited arranging. Right now the colors and textures were a mess, so she took them all out and went to get a hot cup of coffee to help clear her head. Taking a soothing gulp of the magical elixir, she turned her thoughts from Phillip Reynolds toward Rodney's first week back at school.

Susan could hardly believe how well he seemed to be doing. She knew that he had been doing his homework and had even shown Rodney his current grades using the school's website. Rodney had tried to act like it wasn't a big deal, but Susan could feel the pride he seemed to be taking in his accomplishments. Though she had asked him about school, the standard "nothing" was still the answer when it came to her inquiries. Of course, this should have made her feel better, since it seemed the "normal" kind of answer from kids his age.

The tether hadn't alarmed yet, and Susan prayed every day that Rodney could stay on track and put further distance between himself and the kids he used to hang out with in school. One very positive thing was the young woman who had called the house a few times, Veronica. Rodney wouldn't give Susan too much information, but she could tell by the way he quickly took the phone into his room that Veronica was of great interest to her son.

Today would mark the first fully completed week of school since Rodney's suspension. Actually, it would probably be the first week that Rodney had been in school each day, and in class each hour, for longer than Susan knew. Rodney's former drinking, drug use, and poor companion choices had led to many unexcused absences. Sometimes it was a random class period missed a few times a week. Other times there were entire days that Rodney couldn't account for. This week though, he had been there every day, every hour, and even during lunches. As a result of his suspension and past record, Rodney had been limited to closed campus options for lunch, but he hadn't put up the fight Susan had expected. She suspected that Veronica had a great deal to do with that too.

Deciding to give up for the day as she mangled yet another arrangement, Susan locked up the shop and made her way to her car. She was going to create a spectacular dinner to celebrate Rodney's first week, and she needed to stop at the supermarket on the way home. The menu was all planned in her head, but she was going to need some ingredients to move things into the presentation phase.

The parking lot of the local grocery wasn't half filled when Susan pulled in, and she was grateful that it wouldn't be too busy inside. She loved to meander up and down aisles, browsing through the produce and bakery departments, taking her time to enjoy the possibilities of creating something new to share with her family.

Even Joe had loved her cooking Susan remembered, and then stopped as she tried not to revisit that part of her life. She had become expert at altering her memories to include her and the kids without the overshadowing of her ex-husband. Delving into those areas never left her feeling better, just tired and ashamed at the allowances she had given to such evil. She couldn't wish that Joe had never been her husband, though, as that would eliminate Taylor and Rodney from her life as well. No matter how hard Rodney had made things at times, Susan loved both of her children with all of her heart and soul. She would do anything to protect them, and in fact had done everything to protect them, nearly losing her life in the bargain.

Shaking off the bad aura, Susan dug her hands into the bin of fresh green beans, making sure that the vegetables were crisp and not too bendy. Every time she bought fresh green beans, Susan was reminded of her grandmother, who used to sit for hours on the front porch snapping off the ends and breaking them into sections.

She smiled, remembering how much she had loved her grandmother, and how lost she'd felt when she had died at the age of one hundred and two. Even though her grandmother had suffered a stroke in the last year of her life, Susan remembered her vitality, sense of humor, and most of all her strength to survive at all costs.

After Susan's parents had died, it was Grandma who'd taken Susan in and raised her. It was an unconventional parenting style, but Susan's heart had been filled and she'd been sheltered. She'd been so anxious to replace Grandma's warmth that she was easy prey for Joe when he sauntered into her life playing the role of knight in shining armor—a role that quickly vanished once he'd married her and taken her away.

With a deep sigh, she twisted the bag of green beans shut with a metal tie. Susan moved to the meat department, picking up four boneless, skinless chicken breasts for the cordon bleu recipe she was putting together for dinner. She moved slowly through the other aisles, picking up many items just to see what possibilities there might be for future meals. When Susan completed her shopping, she left the store with two large, blue bags filled with the makings of a wonderful meal.

The automatic doors slid open and Susan left, walking into a small group of high-school aged students standing in front, smoking, and generally loitering about the area. With a start, Susan recognized one of the group members, a surly young woman slightly shorter than her own height, with unnaturally black, dirty hair streaked with lines of purple and neon pink. The beauty of her face was marred by a dozen or so piercings that decorated her eyebrows, nose, and lips.

Trying to get past without a confrontation, Susan went to walk around the periphery of the crowd. Suddenly, the pierced girl stepped in front of Susan. The smell of smoke was overwhelming, but Susan decided to avoid a fight and took a positive stance.

"Well, hello. Melinda, isn't it? I thought I recognized you," Susan said in a pleasant voice. She couldn't believe that the store's manager allowed this crowd to hang around and glanced to see if other customers might be approaching.

"Yeah, you're Rodney's mom, right?" Melinda answered angrily. "I saw him back at school this week. Trying to be all goody-two-shoes now is he?"

Susan did not want to banter with this group, so she moved aside and tried to leave. "Well, it was nice talking to you, Melinda," Susan said.

She felt the menacing air of the group as she walked away. Pushing the button to unlock the trunk, Susan quickly set the bags inside and turned to get into her car. Melinda was there, leaning against the driver-side door.

"Excuse me, please," Susan tried, smiling and hoping that the manager might notice the drama unfolding in the parking lot of his store.

Melinda took a long pull on the cigarette she was smoking, grinding the butt down into the pavement with her shoe when she finished. Susan decided that the nice approach wasn't working and stood up tall and strong, motioning for Melinda to move away from the car.

Unexpectedly, Melinda stepped away. As Susan went to get into her car, Melinda laughed. Susan looked at the girl and wondered how her son could have ever wanted to hang out with this girl. She oozed anger and disrespect, and Susan admitted that was probably what had pulled Rodney in. She sent another silent prayer to the gods above that her son would make it work for himself this time and that Rodney would never again be part of a group that found pleasure in tormenting people.

"Is there something else, Melinda?" Susan said firmly.

"Yeah, you tell that stuck-up traitor kid of yours that we know he ratted Alan out and that this ain't over by a long shot." Melinda sneered, turning away and sauntering back to the group.

Shaken to her very core, Susan somehow managed to keep her emotions in check until she drove out of the parking lot. She had no idea what Melinda was referring to, but she was clear about the emotions behind the statement. If they thought that Rodney was a snitch there could be dangerous consequences. She had to wonder if they had been threatening him this whole week. Rodney hadn't said anything, but that was no gauge of what had happened. She knew that she was going to have to contact Phillip. She was also certain she wanted her daughter home. It was time to pull the wagons into protective formation. Susan needed both of her kids close to feel at full strength. In addition, she and Rodney were going to have a talk. It was time for her son to come clean, whether he wanted to tell his mom about it or not.

One thing was certain, Susan thought as she pulled into her driveway. It was not going to be the sweet, cozy meal she had anticipated. She wondered if she should stick with the conventional menu she had planned, or simply go ahead and serve up some spicy jalapeno creation instead. Maybe she would make a flambé for dessert, and beat the fire to the punch. When would her life finally become predictable, routine, or even boring?

20

Rodney left Oxford High School feeling pretty good about his first finished week. He made it quickly to OYC and got to work immediately. He was looking forward to some basketball time after he finished up his cleaning duties, but then was called into a meeting with Mr. Rodriguez. When Rodney was told by one of the other workers that Mr. R wanted to see him in his office, a familiar fear crept into his gut. As he walked through the building, Rodney was busy surveying his behavior of the past two weeks, trying to figure out what he'd done wrong and what kind of trouble he was in for whatever it had been.

Mr. Rodriguez was sitting behind his desk, scowling at the computer screen in front of him. Rodney entered without a word, sitting where Mr. Rodriguez absently waved. Finally, the older man let out a frustrated noise and spun around to face Rodney. Without giving him a chance, Rodney began to speak.

"Look, Mr. Rodriguez, I don't know what I did, but I'm really sorry and I won't let it happen again. I had a decent first week at school, and…" Rodney rushed into an apology.

Mr. Rodriguez sat, finally breaking into a robust laughing fit. "Oh, Rodney," he said, "you do so remind me of myself at your age! Why do you assume I called you here for trouble?" Rodney was stunned. It had never occurred to him that it could be for any other reason.

With a smirk, Rodney shrugged his shoulders, just as Mr. Oakes entered the office. Looking back at Mr. Rodriguez, Rodney said, "Great, see, I must be in serious trouble," and then he and Mr. Rodriguez both laughed as Mr. Oakes's face clouded with confusion.

After explanations were made, Rodney sat and listened as the men explained to Rodney that he had completed his hours of community service required by the court's ruling. Rodney was stunned. He had become so involved with the people and activities at the center that the requirement had been all but forgotten.

Mr. Oakes told Rodney that he'd made great progress and that he was forwarding a letter of recommendation to Judge Garcia about Rodney. Suddenly, Rodney understood why he had been called in here.

"So, you want me to go, right?" he said quietly, finally making the connection.

"Quite the opposite," Mr. Rodriguez stated. "We've been impressed with the job you've done here, Rodney. You've gone above and beyond what we required. You not only completed your studies, but according to Veronica you mastered the curriculum. You not only took on the cleaning responsibilities, but you helped many of our young residents feel more comfortable."

Rodney looked up in surprise as Mr. Rodriguez finished. Mr. Rodriguez raised his eyebrow in the famous "look" known by the staff at the center. "Please, do not think anything happens here that I don't know about, young man. Little Cecelia told me about how you sat with her during her first lunch here; and about the stuffed bear she found on her bed. A late present from Santa is what I believe she said. Really, Santa?" Mr. Rodriguez looked at Rodney with respect.

"Well, she told me last year Santa skipped her house, and she got nothing. She was scared and lonely and I figured…" Rodney let his sentence trail off.

"It was a wonderful act of kindness, Rodney. You gave her more than a bear to hold at night when she's afraid. You gave her the gift of hope, and that will stay with her well past the life of the stuffed animal," he explained.

"So, are you trying to tell me that I get to stay?" Rodney asked. Mr. Oakes shook his head sadly at Mr. Rodriguez.

"See, Thomas," he said sadly, "they seem so smart, and then…" He laughed.

"Yes, we want you to stay on here at Oxford Youth Center, Rodney. Of course, since your hours are completed, you won't be required to volunteer here any longer. The decision is completely up to you, young man."

Rodney leaned back in his seat. "Would it be like a paying job?" he asked, raising his eyebrow in perfect imitation of Mr. Rodriguez's trademark expression.

Both men laughed, and Rodney sat up again, in order to show respect to them. "Sorry, Rodney, I wish the center had the funding to pay you; but as you know, every penny we earn goes to the children here."

"But you're saying that I can keep coming here, and play basketball, and maybe hang out and help the little kids sometimes too?" Rodney had never been given a chance like this, and he certainly didn't want to blow it. It also gave him a better foothold on the track he was trying to force his life into now that he was cleaned up a bit.

"Yes, Rodney. You can come here as often as you'd like to play basketball, play with the kids, help out when you want to as well. But remember, the same rules apply as before. When you're here, you must be respectful; and you cannot be here if you have been using. We cannot have drugs or alcohol around the children. If we feel you're under the influence, you will be asked to leave until you are sober," Mr. Oakes explained.

"Yes, sir. I know. I've been really trying this time. I feel like I'm on a better path now," Rodney said.

"And that's great, Rodney. You know how proud we both are of your progress; but remember that addiction is a daily battle. Our doors are always open to help you, and we would love for you to become a more permanent part of Oxford Youth Center," Mr. Rodriguez finished up.

Rodney stood and reached out to shake Mr. Rodriguez's hand. "Thank you, sir, for everything. I accept your offer, and if it's all right with you I am now going to do my best to stomp some of the other guys in a friendly game of three-on-three basketball."

"Excellent, Rodney," Mr. Oakes said, standing up and shaking his hand as well. "Remember, play by the rules," he added.

"Of course. It's actually kind of a homework assignment," Rodney added chuckling. "We just started a basketball unit in gym class this week, so I need to hone my skills if I'm going to win the trophy." Rodney's eyes sparkled as he recalled the trophy: his hideous, gaudy goal.

He left the office walking on air, and then spent the next hour sweating it out with the new friends he'd made while serving his community hours the last few weeks. Three weeks ago he had been sitting in jail, hating life, his mother, and the world in general. Now, he felt a world away from that place as he walked home, looking forward to a hot shower and a great dinner with his mom. He didn't even mind that he was going to have homework to do this weekend. Rodney wanted to show Mrs. Rule how much he was capable of in her class and had decided that if she didn't grade him fairly, he would fight the system. Plus, good grades would impress Veronica, and since she was no longer officially his tutor, Rodney felt the door had opened for them to be more than just friends.

Yep, Rodney was feeling pretty good right now. As he walked, he began to whistle, looking forward to new standings as a student, with a gorgeous girlfriend, and a parent at home who had given him another chance even when he didn't deserve it. He didn't even mind the presence of the tether too much anymore, seeing it as a safeguard if he wanted to do something stupid. Knowing the consequences helped Rodney keep out of trouble this time around. His whistling grew more boisterous as he contemplated the possibilities his life held now that he had come clean. The dusky evening wrapped him in a cloak of protectiveness. He finished his walk toward the delicious scents of baking chicken and cherry flambé, unaware of what awaited him.

21

Susan heard whistling from outside in the darkness, and flipped on the porch light just in time to see Rodney shutting the picket-fence gate as he came up their walk. She still hadn't decided if she should warn Rodney about Melinda's threat and wanted to talk to Phillip first. Susan watched her son come up the path and realized that Rodney seemed happy and at ease. It was something she had missed for so long that recognizing it hit her like a physical blow.

Rodney came in the door and saw tears in his mother's eyes. "Mom, what's wrong?" he said rushing over to her.

"Nothing." Susan laughed, wiping her eyes with the tissue she pulled from her pocket.

"Mom, you're crying!" Rodney said, suddenly worried.

"I'm being silly," Susan explained. "I just realized that you seem really happy, and it made me happy to see you so happy, and then I started crying, and that's when you came in and saw me, so…" she blathered on in reply.

Rodney shook his head in mock sympathy. "You women. I will never understand you," he said and moved away quickly as Susan tried to snap him with the dishtowel.

"Dinner will be ready in about half an hour you goof," Susan said, wiping the remaining moisture from her eyes.

"Good, so I have time to take a shower? I was playing basketball, and I'm pretty smelly," he added, moving in and blowing his smell toward her.

"Please! Shower!" Susan laughed and watched him run upstairs.

Deciding that this was as good a time as any, Susan picked up the phone and dialed the number that Phillip had given her in case she needed to contact him about Rodney. His voicemail came on immediately, so she left a brief message about what had happened in the grocery lot, trying not to sound too dramatic.

Next, while she was feeling courageous, Susan dialed Taylor's number. She hadn't talked to Taylor since the night of Rodney's last arrest. Taylor had not hesitated to express her disgust at Rodney's behavior and had told Susan enough was enough. If it had been up to Taylor, Rodney would have been shipped to the juvenile detention center that night. As Taylor had put it, "Do not pass go, send him directly to jail, Mom. Just like when we used to play that game." Though Susan had understood Taylor's reaction, she also knew that Rodney was worthy of another chance.

Taylor had been irritated and told Susan she was sure to regret her decision. Taylor's parting comment had been to tell Susan to call her back when Rodney got busted again, which she was sure would be all too quickly.

Susan had called and left a message after Rodney's first few days home, but had purposely called when she knew Taylor would be at work. Susan's feelings were still too raw to have them trampled, so she kept her daughter in the loop from a distance. Tonight, however, was different. Rodney had completed three weeks, tested clean each week, and brought up his grades.

Taylor's phone rang twice and then Susan heard her daughter's voice on the other end of the line. "Hey, Mom," Taylor said. "You're calling when you know I'm home. Does that mean Rodney blew it already?"

"Hello, and no, your brother has had an outstanding three weeks. Taylor, he's like the old Rodney," Susan said, unable to keep the pride out of her voice.

Rodney passed the upstairs hallway on his way to the shower and heard his mother's voice. Knowing it was wrong, but unable to move on quite yet, Rodney stood outside the open bathroom door and listened to his mother's end of the conversation.

"Really, Taylor, I know that you had doubts, but Rodney seems to be working so hard this time. I mean, he hasn't missed a day at school, not even one class. All of his drug drops have been clean. He's even making new friends at school and the center where he's been doing his community service hours."

Rodney was stunned at the pride he heard in his mom's voice. He wasn't surprised that his sister had doubted his ability to clean up his act. He was even willing to admit that she'd had some good reasons to doubt. However, he had done a great job so far, and his mom was feeling the love from the way she was gushing to Taylor about him. Rodney couldn't deny that the idea of his mom telling Taylor how great she thought he was fueled his ego. Taylor, as far as Rodney could see, had always been the favorite. Taylor always did well in school, had good friends, and never skipped school or did any of the stupid tricks he'd done. Taylor was the typical teacher's pet that Rodney found himself despising in school. But now, he was on the top of mom's list, and he was finding that he liked the position.

Deciding he'd heard enough and could now get into the shower, Rodney froze as he heard his mother's next remarks.

"So, yes, sweetheart, I was hoping that you could come home for a visit soon. It has been such a long time, Taylor, and I think Rodney would be glad to see you too." Rodney waited for the familiar pain that accompanied the idea of his sister visiting, and waited, and waited, but it didn't strike him as he stood there. Maybe be really was changing, he thought to himself, closing the door behind him silently. The pounding of hot water soon washed over him, and Rodney let his mind shut down and simply enjoyed the good feeling. Maybe he really was changing.

22

An hour later, Rodney and his mother sat around the remains of another delicious meal. "That was awesome, Mom," Rodney said, rubbing his full stomach. "So, what's for dessert?" He laughed as Susan sighed dramatically.

"Cherry flambé," she said, knowing he would be impressed. "Do me a favor, and grab the grill lighter from outside, please?" she asked, setting dirty dishes inside the sink and moving to take the flambé from the refrigerator. She'd tried to get Rodney to talk about his week at school, but he hadn't shared much. After a bit of pushing, he'd finally talked about his meeting with Mr. Rodriguez. Susan had left it at that, afraid to ruin the evening.

Her phone rang just as Rodney walked outside to the grill, and she would have ignored it, except it was Phillip. She answered quickly, and whispered, "Hello, this is Susan."

"Susan! I'm sorry it took so long to get back to you. I've been involved with a situation, and I just got back into town," Phillip explained. Susan felt relief, knowing Phillip would help with Rodney and also that her behavior hadn't chased this man away.

"Thank you, Phillip. I only have a minute. There's something very important I need to talk to you about, but Rodney is on his way back in from outside, and I don't want him to hear me," she raced to explain as Rodney came whistling back, waving the long-stemmed lighter like a sword.

Susan smiled at Rodney playfully and took the lighter from him. She motioned to the refrigerator for Rodney to get the dessert and place it on the table.

Phillip's years of reading nuances wasn't wasted, as he heard Susan's explanation. "Okay, so you can't talk right now, but you need to as soon as possible," Phillip said.

Noncommittally, Susan responded, "Yes, that's right." She was hoping that Phillip would understand, but didn't want to jeopardize her shaky relationship with Rodney by filling him in quite yet.

"I could come over. Say in an hour?" Phillip said.

"No, that won't work. My son is doing homework, and I don't want to disturb him," she said evasively. Rodney gave her a questioning look, and Susan rolled her eyes as if she were talking to a telemarketer.

"We can meet at the station or somewhere in town. You're also welcome to come here," Phillip suggested.

"I think the last option is best," Susan said.

"I'll text you the address and if you need directions just call me and I'll get you here. Is that okay?"

"Yes, that will be fine. Thanks so much for calling during *our* dinner hour. Perhaps next time I can call *your* house?" Susan ended, hoping that Phillip caught on to her alibi.

Hanging up the phone, she turned to Rodney, flipping off the light switch as she did so. "Dramatic effect," Susan said, as she handed Rodney the lighter. Rodney's eyes lit up like he was five and being offered the cake beaters. "Would you do the honors of lighting the flambé?" she asked, already knowing the answer.

Rodney clicked on the lighter and looked at Susan. Before he placed the flame to the brandy-filled dessert, he looked her straight in the eyes. "Thanks, Mom, for everything the last few weeks. I know it isn't easy to love me sometimes."

Susan reached out and turned off the lighter. "Rodney, it is always easy to *love* you. I have never stopped loving you for a single moment; and I have never been as proud of you as I am tonight. I know the last few weeks have been rough, but you've done such a great job. I am so glad you're my son," Susan finished, not bothering to wipe away the tears that were rolling down her face. "Now, light this bugger up!" She laughed.

Rodney once again lit the flame, smiling over at Susan before he turned back to the cherry dessert, setting the brandy alight with a burst of foot-high flames. Mother and son stood silently, watching the liquid burn down so they could enjoy the heated delight. Susan stepped closer to Rodney and wrapped her arms around his shoulders.

"I love you, Rodney," she whispered into the dark room.

"I love you too, Mom," Rodney whispered back almost too quietly to be heard. Susan smiled, because she *had* heard it and because she knew it was true. Now, if she could just figure out how to protect this boy she loved from Melinda and her threats.

Pushing it aside for her conversation with Phillip, Susan dished out the dessert and ate in the quiet darkness with Rodney. She would figure it out. She had protected her children from danger in the past, and this time would be no different.

23

Susan explained to Rodney that she had some errands to run and then asked if he would be okay if she left him alone for an hour or two. Rodney had assured her, with a shake of his tethered leg, that he wouldn't be going out that night. Susan set the home alarm just before leaving, and she knew that if one outside door or window was opened even a crack she would be alerted. With Melinda's threat fresh in her mind, Susan didn't want to leave Rodney in the house, but she needed to talk to Phillip, and she needed privacy to do it properly.

Less than ten minutes later, Susan found herself driving slowly down Old Hawk Road, looking at the mailbox numbers at the end of the long driveways. The houses here were hidden from the road's view by trees that stood strong and solid. Susan hadn't expected Phillip to live in such a wealthy area in Oxford, and she chastised herself for her stereotyping.

Phillip stepped out onto his front porch as Susan's car stopped at the peak of the circular driveway. "Some digs," she said to him as she shut the door and moved forward.

"Years of embezzling!" He laughed and then quickly corrected, "I'm only kidding, you know! Actually, my family used to own most of this forest, but times changed, Great-Grandpa sold the land, and now this is all that's left of the Reynolds' family fortune." Phillip laughed, but Susan detected a trace of regret in the telling.

"So, I'm not the only one with a secret past after all, hmm?" she teased to lighten the tension in Phillip's face.

He smiled at her as he took her elbow and led her into the large, open hallway of his home. The outside was shadowed by darkness, but Susan thought it was finished in a woodsy tone that continued into the interior. She was struck by the simplicity of the floor plan that made the furnishings and decorations placed around the room more powerful. There was a wide staircase that moved up to the second floor on her left. Susan could see one hallway above with a few closed doors.

As Phillip took her coat and hung it on the rack that stood next to the front door, Susan peeked around him into the large living room. Directly in the center of the room was a large oak-mantled fireplace roaring with a burning fire. Susan instinctively moved into the warmth of the room. The furniture was large and almost begged her to sit down and rest. The warm, deep, dark chocolate color was clearly masculine, yet very inviting. All of the end tables were big and made of a lovely maple colored wood, and Susan was drawn toward a rocking chair set near the fireplace. The quilt that rested on the back of the rocker was clearly old, and as Susan looked more closely, she could tell that it had been hand stitched.

"Family heirloom?" she asked, turning to see Phillip standing very still and watching a few feet from her.

"My great-grandmother sewed that for her wedding chest," he explained, moving closer to gently touch the quilt with obvious reverence.

"It's really amazing," said Susan, suddenly very aware of how close Phillip was to her in the room. "My grandma was quite a quilter as well, and this makes me think of the times she tried to teach me."

Phillip sensed the change in her mood, and took a step back from Susan. "Would you like some coffee?" he offered.

"Well, normally yes, but if I have it now I will never get to bed tonight," Susan laughed.

Phillip didn't say anything but gave Susan a look that sent heat racing through her body. Neither of them said anything, and Susan feared for a moment that she would either burst into flame or melt where she stood.

It took willpower, but Phillip stayed where he was and just waited. He had left Susan's shop Monday morning clearly intending to find her again as soon as possible. It had been a long time since he'd been attracted to a woman like he was to Susan Birge, and he didn't want to scare her away.

Sensing that Susan was struggling too, Phillip took the opportunity to assist. One step forward, one and a half back, he thought, knowing that if it was right he could have Susan in his life when it was meant to happen.

"You said you had something important regarding Rodney?" he prompted. He could see the air leave Susan just a bit, and then the fear that filled her eyes.

"God, you must think I'm a horrible person. I almost forgot why I was here," she said, clearly upset.

"Tell me," Phillip said, motioning for her to sit in the large, comfortable chair. He put himself on the couch. He sat close but not too close so that Susan could tell her story. As Susan began to relate her information, the horror of what could possibly be brewing for her son seemed to hit her full force.

Phillip listened, interrupting with a question here or there, but allowing Susan full reign with the details and information.

"So, I tried to see what Rodney knew about this, but I can't be sure if he really doesn't know or if he's just blocking me out like most kids his age seem to do to their parents." Susan finished with a shrug. "He's working so hard to get back on track. Now all I can think about is one of these hoodlums coming after my son."

Phillip had listened and knew that the situation could be serious. "Susan, I wish I could tell you it wasn't a true threat, but this group that Rodney hung out with was filled with some serious criminals in the making."

Susan sighed. She had known that Rodney had been running with a bad crowd even from the small amount of time that she had spent with them. They never hung around her place much, as Susan had made it clear that they would not be allowed to smoke, drink, or do drugs on her watch. Rodney had spent hours screaming at her about how unfair she was and how it was better if they were at home instead of out running the streets. Susan had agreed and told Rodney his friends were welcome, as long as they followed the rules she had set out for all of them.

Phillip interrupted her thoughts with another question. "So, does Rodney know about Melinda's threat today?"

"No!" Susan answered quickly. "I wanted to talk to you first, to see if there was any merit to what Melinda said to me. I just kind of hinted around with Rodney over our dinner as to anything that might be happening at school this week."

"The student Melinda referred to, Alan, he and Rodney were pretty tight, right?" Phillip asked her. He could see Susan's concern and wanted to get as much information as possible.

"Yes. Alan was in the car with Rodney when he got busted the last time at school, but he took off before the police showed up and arrested Rodney. I know that Rodney was terrified that first day back to school about what would happen when he saw Alan. It seemed that there hasn't been any confrontation. I wasn't expecting the attack from Melinda today, but now I'm scared to death!" Susan sat wringing her hands, clearly distressed. Phillip reached over and took her hands in his, offering reassurance through the simple touch.

"We'll get to the bottom of this, Susan, so please try not to worry," he earnestly told her. "I can dig into this further tomorrow from work, but you should know that many of Rodney's old crew got busted shortly before he returned to school. There was a big drug raid, just like we have every year at some point. We bring in the search dogs, and even though you'd think the kids would have learned, we always catch some offenders."

Susan was listening intently. Rodney hadn't shared any of this information with Susan and neither had the school's office. Susan stood up, pacing in frustration.

"Well, don't you think that someone from school should have told me about this? I mean, my kid returns to school right after there's a drug raid, a bunch of his former friends get busted, and no one thought it might be important for me to know?"

"Susan, I know this is frustrating, but I promise I'll do everything possible to make this manageable. If you want to file a complaint against Melinda you can, but at this point there's not much we can do," Phillip explained. This was where it got complicated for people. He knew that if Susan filed the complaint it would certainly fuel the anger of the crew. It might allow her a personal protection order, but an order could be useless in deferring an attack if someone was truly bent on vengeance.

"I don't know, Phillip. Let me talk to Rodney about it tonight or tomorrow morning and see what he's willing to share with me about the whole situation," Susan asked, glancing at her watch.

"You need to go," he said, disappointment clearly in his voice.

"Not quite yet, but soon," she answered. "I'm sure Rodney can't get out of the house without setting off my alarm system, but I would feel better knowing no one else is getting in either."

"Would you like to see the rest of the house then?" Phillip asked. He had noticed Susan looking around earlier, and he took pride in sharing his family's history with visitors.

Susan smiled and nodded, following as Phillip led her back into the entry and then toward the back of his home, where the large kitchen was always a point of pride. The marble countertop lent itself to imaginings of rolling out cookies and large Sunday dinners surrounded by family. "It's so big, and yet so cozy," she said in wonder.

"We used to spend every holiday here, until my parents passed away a few years ago," Phillip told her, never taking his eyes off of Susan. "Now, my sister and her family usually stay out west, so it's just me and Tubs."

"Where is Tubs, by the way?" Susan said, looking around.

Phillip sighed. "I'm embarrassed by the slothness of my version of man's best friend, but since you asked..." he said, leading

Susan up the stairway. When they reached the top of the stairs, Phillip shook his head sadly and opened up the first door. "The master bedroom," he said stepping aside.

In the middle of a thickly quilted bedspread lay the largest lump of dog Susan had ever seen. When she entered, the dog barely opened an eye in greeting. Susan walked over and sat down next to Tubs, scratching behind his large, floppy ear. The dog's tail began to thump strongly against the bed in pleasure.

Phillip stood in the doorway. "He likes you," he said.

Susan realized she was practically lying across Phillip's bed and stood up quickly. Tubs turned his head in protest, whining loudly. "Sorry, bud, I have to go," Susan said, walking past Phillip and making her way back down the staircase.

Phillip looked back at Tubs who had slumped back down as soon as Susan had gotten up. "Great, my dog has gotten further with the woman of my dreams than I have," he muttered. Tubs let out a huge yawn in response, before closing his eyes and going back to sleep.

Trotting down the stairs, Phillip reached Susan as she was putting her coat on. Phillip helped her with the sleeves. "Susan, you don't need to worry about this tonight. I'm sure Melinda was just trying to scare you," he added trying to ease Susan's mind before she headed home.

"Well, it worked," Susan admitted as she fixed her collar and moved toward the front door. "Thank you though, Phillip," she said and without thinking placed her open-palmed hand against his rough cheek. He hadn't shaved since returning home, though she could tell that he had showered before she had arrived. She'd been breathing in his fresh woodsy cologne since walking in the door, and it was playing crazy on her nerves.

"I think I'm going to kiss you now, Susan, if it's all right with you," Phillip said very quietly, afraid to startle her. After an almost imperceptible nod of her head, Susan watched with eyes wide open as Phillip leaned down and stopped a hairsbreadth away from her lips. As a sigh escaped her, Phillip leaned down and gently placed his lips on Susan's, a kiss so soft it was barely felt; but Susan felt it clearly throughout her body. The kiss set off her senses with a need so great that she could barely stand. Feeling her reaction, Phillip deepened the kiss, wrapping his arms around her waist and pulling her full length up against his own body. Without hesitation, Susan wrapped her arms up and around Phillip's neck, her fingers finding grip in his thick, dark hair. The kiss seemed to go on forever, but only lasted a few minutes before Phillip pulled back.

"Wow," Susan whispered, her eyes on Phillip's own dilated eyes.

"I knew it was going to be like that," he said to her. "Now, you'd better go or I won't be able to let you leave tonight," he said huskily.

Susan smiled, a slow, sultry invitation, and spun slowly on her heel motioning for Phillip to stay on the porch. "Good," he heard her say once she was safely out of his reach. As Susan pulled away from his front porch, she looked in her rearview mirror to see Phillip watching her as she left.

It had been a most educational evening after all, she thought to herself as she made the short drive home to her waiting son. Rodney was safely in his room, sleeping on his bed with math problems spread around him. It seemed so normal that for a moment Susan was almost able to forget what might be brewing around her family.

She was diligent about checking the alarm system and the locks on the doors before heading up to her own bedroom. She was going to have to trust Phillip to help her, and she was hoping it was the right decision. She fell asleep with Phillip's kiss still on her lips, her body humming with unfulfilled needs he'd awakened. She knew that in the morning she would need to confront Rodney with questions and that it could lead to an ugly scene, but it couldn't be avoided. If Rodney was going to change, he was going to have to learn to trust too.

Susan sighed and rolled up into a ball, looking for sleep that took over quickly. Her dreams were filled with monsters and knights in shining armor and princesses who were able to save themselves but who also knew when to accept assistance to slay the dragons.

24

Susan was jolted awake the next morning to the screeching of the house's alarm system. It had broken through the nightmare where she'd been fighting in hand-to-hand battle with a terrifyingly large Cyclops. The events of the day before came back and she feared with all her heart that someone had come for Rodney. She jumped out of bed and grabbed the baseball bat she kept hidden beside her bed.

Running down the stairs, she began screaming, "Get out of my house!" She knew the alarm company would have already responded to the alarm, but Susan attacked with a mother's rage. Still unable to see who had broken in, she screamed again. "Do you hear me? Get OUT of my house and leave my son alone!"

Rodney walked in the front door holding the day's mail and Susan nearly took his head off with the bat. "Mom! What the hell?" he yelled, ducking as Susan backed off at the same time.

"Oh my gosh, honey, I'm so sorry! I thought someone had broken in," she said as she collapsed onto the couch.

"Seriously? I just went out for the mail, and the stupid system went off. Since when do you set it while we're actually here?" Rodney asked. He was looking at Susan as if she'd lost her mind.

Susan held up a finger to check Rodney's questioning and got up to call the alarm company. Once she had the incident resolved, she returned to her son. Rodney was holding the baseball bat in his hands, shaking his head at her and chuckling. "I've got to give it to you, Mom," he said. "That was one hell of a swing!"

"No cussing," she said, laughing and taking the bat back from Rodney.

"So, what's the deal with setting the alarm during the day?" he asked again. "Oh, wait a minute. You set it in case I tried to leave, didn't you? Haven't I earned back even a little of your trust yet, Mom?" Rodney asked, clearly hurt.

"That isn't it," she said. "Sit down, and I'll tell you why I locked up the house." Susan could see insecurity and defensiveness written on Rodney's face and felt bad. She needed to get some answers, though, and Rodney was currently the most reliable source.

"Son, listen to me. What can you tell me about the crew? Melinda and the others?" she asked softly.

Rodney turned his head away from her, a move that screamed of evasive answers. Susan was too familiar with how to spot a lie, and no eye contact was a clear sign. "I haven't seen them, if that's what you're asking me," he answered after looking her straight in the eye.

"That wasn't what I was asking, Rodney. Look, I need you to come clean with me so that I can help you, protect you, from what might be happening," Susan said, tears filling her eyes against her will.

"Protect me from what, Mom? Alan and a bunch of kids apparently got busted at school last week. Veronica told me there was some big raid, and a ton of kids got nailed. How stupid could they be? I mean, the cops come through every year around this time with the dogs." When he realized what he had basically admitted, he looked away from Susan, dropping his head.

Susan reached over and took Rodney's hands in her own. "Honey, I am not accusing you of anything. It's just that, well, I saw Melinda yesterday in town."

Rodney's head shot up quickly. "What do you mean, you saw her? What did you do, Mom?"

"What did I do? Why would that be your first question, Rodney?" Susan asked, starting to worry at the familiar track of the conversation. This is how it had always been in the past. Susan would try to help, Rodney became defensive, and it would end in him storming out mad and making threats. For a number of reasons, Susan didn't want that to happen today. She was worried about her son's safety with the crew, but she didn't want him storming away and setting off the tether either. If he stayed out of trouble for another week or so, the court would be removing the tether. That was when Rodney's resolve to stay on the straight and narrow would be tested in earnest.

Susan watched Rodney take a deep breath. "Mom, you don't know what Melinda is really like. If you piss her off," he began and stopped as Susan mouthed the words *no cussing* at him and smiled. "If you irritate her, well, you just don't know what she might do." Susan felt cold dread squeeze her heart.

"I don't suppose you'd be willing to be more specific?" she asked, already knowing that he wouldn't tell her more. Rodney shook his head, affirming her suspicions.

"Just trust me, okay?" he asked staring directly at her once again. "I mean, she must have given you the creeps if you set the alarm like you did."

"There's more to it than that," Susan said. She then related the entire incident from the time she'd left the store until she had called Phillip. Susan also filled him in with what she had learned from Phillip, choosing to leave out the more personal details of her visit.

Rodney was looking more upset by the minute, but Susan knew that he needed to know exactly what was going on to be able to deal with it properly.

"So, I need to know the truth, Rodney. If you know anything about this that might help us get to the bottom of Melinda's story, it would be a big help. Why would she think you'd ratted them out if you weren't even there? You weren't allowed to be hanging out with them, and I know you haven't these last few weeks. So, any ideas why Melinda would think that you're involved?" Susan asked again. She wanted answers, but she was also desperately hoping that Rodney knew nothing about the whole situation.

"I have not talked to any of them since Alan ditched and ran. I don't know, maybe he's the one making them think I snitched. Maybe it's his way of making sure I don't retaliate against him for leaving me to hang alone. I don't know, Mom. I mean, it isn't like the things Melinda goes off on usually have a solid backing in reason," Rodney said.

"So, she's a crazy hot head, is what you're telling me," Susan summed up. "And the crew follows her lead. If they all want to believe you're involved, we're going to need some help."

"Pretty much sounds like it," Rodney said.

"Okay, well I'm going to call Phil…Officer Reynolds and fill him in. Then I'm going to take a long shower. I would like it if you could stick around the house please?" Rodney gave her a look so reminiscent of his childhood faces that Susan started to laugh. "I know, you're not a baby, but I'll feel better knowing that you're inside while I get ready. Humor your old mother, okay?" she added with another smile.

She walked away and up the stairs to call Phillip, smiling as she realized that this was the first confrontation in many months that had ended in a positive way. Rodney had begun to change, and that was something good to hang on to now.

However, across town Melinda did not share that sentiment as she sneered in twisted delight devising a plan to teach Rodney that leaving her would not be so simple.

25

Rodney watched his mom walk up the stairs to call the local police. He hadn't missed the slip up when she had called Officer Reynolds by his first name. He was pretty sure that cop had been eyeballing his mom. Rodney couldn't remember his mom ever giving a man a second glance. Sure, she got a number of double takes when they were out and about. He had never been afraid to admit that his mom was in the hot category; it was just never an issue since she'd never dated. There hadn't been anyone since his dad, and Rodney remembered how he used to make believe.

His favorite scenario was the one where he and his mom were walking somewhere together. They stopped for ice cream and out of the blue his father would appear. His mom would stop what she was doing and fall into his dad's arms. Then, they all came back and lived happily ever after. The ending was always the same, no matter how the story began time and time again. Rodney knew it was stupid, but he had read somewhere that no matter how old a kid was he still wished for his parents to get back together again. At least that had been one area that he had been like the 'normal' kids, he thought.

Now there was this mess to deal with, just when Rodney felt like he was getting clear of the crew. If Melinda was nervy enough to approach his mom, there was no telling what else might happen with them. He would never tell his mom, but he was actually relieved that she was going to involve the police in this one. Having run with the crew for the last year and a half or

133

so, Rodney knew what they were capable of, and he didn't like being on the receiving end of their vengeance.

Not much later, there was a knock on the door, and Rodney watched his mom come downstairs, all showered and made-up like she was going somewhere special. She moved to the door and let in Officer Reynolds. Rodney stayed where he was, to watch the interaction of his mom and the local cop. Sure enough, Officer Reynolds was all smiles as he watched his mom move toward the doorway and let him inside the house. Rodney couldn't help the jolt of anger, as he thought about his mom having an interest in someone, especially since it was the officer who had arrested him not a month earlier.

"Susan, I've got some news for you," Rodney heard the officer say to his mom.

"Thank you, Phillip," his mom said, turning to call Rodney over to them at the kitchen table.

"Can I get you something to drink?" she asked, encompassing both Rodney and Phillip in her look.

"No thanks," they answered at the same time.

"Rodney, nice to see you again," Officer Reynolds said as he reached over to shake his hand. "Your mom has been telling me how well you've done the last few weeks. She's very proud of you." He took a seat at the table as Rodney's mom sat down.

"Seems like the two of you have had quite a bit of time to talk, huh?" Rodney said in a rather accusing voice.

"Rodney!" his mother interjected quickly. "Officer Reynolds has been a great support the last few weeks. In fact, he came all the way over here just to help us with the 'Melinda' situation. So, be nice please." His mother gave him the look that in the past might have fueled Rodney's rage but today just made him feel like a stupid, jealous, little boy.

"Yeah, sorry," Rodney said. "I'm just cranked up about Melinda threatening my mom. I really don't know what to do, well, without getting back into trouble at least," Rodney added for the benefit of everyone at the table. He wanted to make sure they both knew he was trying his best to stay on track. Veronica had made it clear that she wasn't going to hang out with a hoodlum, tutor or not. Plus, there were the people down at OYC now too.

Officer Reynolds turned toward Rodney. "Well, I think the first thing we need to do is get you and your mom to file personal protection orders, which should be easy to do based on the threat Melinda made on Friday afternoon." Rodney couldn't help scoffing at the idea of a PPO. He knew no piece of paper was going to keep his mom safe from Melinda.

Rodney's mom was watching him, and she had gone pale. "Mom, what's wrong," he asked, afraid of the look on her face.

"Nothing, honey. I'm fine," his mom said, but even Officer Reynolds was looking at her with concern. Rodney watched as Reynolds's hand moved forward to cover his mother's, but then pulled back as he realized they were being watched.

"Are you okay, Susan?"

Rodney's mom straightened up a bit and smiled. It was such a forced effort that Rodney became even more concerned than he'd been a few minutes ago. "I'm fine," she said again. "So, do we need to go down to the station for the orders?" she asked.

"Yes, that would be easiest. Plus, while you're down there, we can get more information for the report. None of the crew came out unscathed in the raid at school. Their files are getting thicker each day. The more Rodney can tell us, the quicker we might be able to shut down whatever it is they're planning," he said, directing his full attention at Rodney.

"Wait a minute!" Rodney said. "I'm good with the protection orders, and whatever I need to do to help Mom be safe, but I never said I was going to turn into a snitch," Rodney proclaimed.

"Rodney, if it will help stop what they're planning, then you need to help the police. I'm in over my head here, son," he heard his mom beg.

Just as Rodney was about to lose his cool, the sound of a car pulling up was heard outside in the driveway. Even though it was a cool autumn day, they usually left the kitchen window open for the fresh air until it was absolutely too cold. Officer Reynolds was on his feet before Rodney could get up and grab the baseball bat that had been left leaning against the stairway.

"Oh, for Heaven's sake," he heard his mother say. "It isn't like they're going to drive up in the middle of the day and knock on the door before trying to beat up my son!" she said, finding humor in the protective stances of the two men in the kitchen. Rodney watched his mom move around him and Officer Reynolds and then watched her face transform into pure joy.

Before he could ask for an explanation, his mom yelled out, "Taylor! Taylor! I didn't know you were coming!" She was out the door, engulfing the rather tall, slender young woman who was his sister in a gigantic hug. Rodney was shocked. What the hell was Taylor doing here? Obviously his mother had called her, but Rodney couldn't imagine why Taylor had decided to take her up on a visit. She'd adamantly refused so many times before.

Rodney felt the old jealousy rushing through his veins. Taylor had always been the golden child, doing well in school, making friends with the good kids, never fighting and instead trying to keep the peace. Most of all, Rodney's blood roiled with the knowledge that Taylor had memories of time spent with their dad, and no matter how hard he tried, Rodney had nothing of his father tucked in his brain.

Just as the pain of this passed over his face, Taylor looked up and saw Rodney watching them. She flinched as if she'd been slapped, and Rodney frowned. He used to be so good at keeping emotions from his expression. The last month had changed him more than he'd realized.

Trying to ease the tension, Rodney pleasantly called out, "Hey there, Sis. Nice surprise." Taylor smiled and moved beside their mom, walking toward the house with her arm around her shoulder. *She's like a younger version of Mom,* Rodney thought as he watched them together.

As they came to the door, Taylor looked at Officer Reynolds and then to Rodney. A look of disgust shuddered through her as she asked Rodney, "So, up to your old tricks again, little brother?"

"Why don't you…" Rodney began and was then promptly interrupted by the police officer in question.

"Taylor, I'm Phillip Reynolds. Though I'm here at the moment on official business, it's geared toward a matter your brother is assisting my department in." Taylor looked from Rodney over to where their mom was smiling at everyone in the room. Rodney saw his mom grin and nod at Taylor in confirmation.

"Hmm, well what a nice change, Rodney. So, what's going on then?" Taylor asked seriously. Rodney listened as his mom filled his sister in briefly with the main details of the situation.

"Gee, Mom," Taylor said. "Why don't you two head down to the station then, and I'll bring in my bag and unpack. I'd planned on staying for about a week, but if you need me longer just tell me. I can make new arrangements without too much trouble," Taylor offered, and again Rodney was struck with how together his sister's life always seemed. As far as he was concerned, Taylor had never really known how hard survival could be, and that's why she was always on top of her game. Rodney was sure that if he'd been able to spend more time with his dad his life would have been easier too.

His mom had been watching him since Taylor arrived, and seemed to feel the tension. "Are you sure, Taylor? I feel horrible leaving as soon as you get here," his mom said. Rodney had a feeling that his mom was anxious to leave. First of all, it would be better to have the protection orders in case Melinda tried to come onto the property. More importantly now, as Rodney was reading it, leaving would put some distance between him and his sister.

Officer Reynolds was soon escorting Rodney and his mom to the squad car, a bit too eager to spend more time with his mom as far as he was concerned. Rodney sat in the back. Watching the house disappear in the rearview mirror gave him a chill of déjà vu that left him more concerned than he wanted to admit. It weirded him out sitting back here, even though he knew he wasn't in any trouble. He slumped back against the seat trying not to notice that Officer Reynolds had taken his mother's hand as they left.

26

Susan was exhausted by the time Phillip dropped her back off at the house with Rodney. She stayed by the car for a minute after Rodney sulked inside, watching her son look back and stare a moment longer than necessary before he slammed into the house. Phillip immediately put his arms around Susan and pulled her into a hug. Susan knew her body was humming with the stress of the afternoon.

She didn't care if the neighbors were watching. Susan had realized that completely closing down her own life was not healthy. She had moved away from her past with Joe Birge. She would never heal fully as long as she locked her heart away. At some point she would have to trust someone again.

It had gone worse than she'd imagined at the station. Rodney had answered general questions about the crew, but would not give any specific details about activities while he'd been with them. Susan had begged, pleaded, and finally cried in frustration, but Rodney wouldn't budge.

Now Susan had two crisp personal protection orders in her purse. She knew from her past these would do nothing to stop someone in a fit of rage. The benefit of the orders was purely to have something in place to prosecute if they should try to come after Rodney. Susan hoped it wouldn't be needed, but at the same time the orders were better than nothing.

"Hey," she heard Phillip whisper. "Where'd you go?" he asked, as he nuzzled her neck with his day's worth of stubble.

"Sorry, totally daydreaming about the papers in my purse," she admitted.

"Please try not to worry," Phillip said reassuringly. "I know you're going to be busy with your daughter here, but I want you to know that I haven't forgotten the other night." Susan felt him pull her just a tiny bit closer to him and sighed in pleasure. With a little growl, Phillip gently pushed her away and toward her front door. He could see Taylor standing and watching them, and would swear she was grinning. Susan sighed deeply and turned back to Phillip.

"Keep sighing like that," he groaned, leaving the statement unfinished.

Susan tried to straighten her expression into something more serious. She failed miserably and decided to enjoy the feeling instead. "See you later, Officer Reynolds," she said coyly over her shoulder, shutting the picket gate behind her with a click of the latch.

"Yes, you will, Ms. Birge," Phillip said in the same tone of voice, getting back into the car and giving the siren a small 'whoop' at Susan's retreating figure. She didn't turn around, but he saw her head drop back in laughter as she entered the house.

Phillip vowed to deal with the Melinda situation as quickly as possible. Based on Rodney's behavior at the station this needed settling immediately, or Rodney wouldn't be able to hold onto his new path.

Susan watched from the window inside the kitchen as Phillip backed out onto the main road, driving away slowly. He waved, and she felt her face split into another large smile.

"So...tell me everything!" Taylor said loudly from the doorway between the kitchen and dining room. "How long has that gorgeous morsel of man been enamored with my mother?" Susan blushed deep, dark red from her hairline to her toes.

"Oh, Officer Reynolds? He's just helping me with Rodney, honey," she tried denying. Susan turned and saw her grown daughter, twenty-four years old, holding her own in the world of finance, and with experiences that left them unable to be anything but honest with each other.

Taylor laughed at Susan's attempt at innocence and then sat down at the small, cozy table. "Spill it, Mom!" she demanded, pushing the chair opposite her out for Susan to sit in and begin talking.

"Well, he is kind of good looking, isn't he?" Susan laughed, brushing the hair from her eyes. She then proceeded to tell Taylor about the whole business. Taylor listened, taking everything in, and occasionally giving Susan feedback. Her eyebrows raised in disbelief when Susan told her about coming home the other night from Phillip's forest home having nothing to show for it but a heart-stopping kiss. Susan ignored the skeptical look on her daughter's face and finished retelling the events of the weeks.

"And then you showed up, surprising me with your beautiful self!" Susan finished, reaching across the table to take Taylor's hands in her own.

Taylor turned and looked up the stairs, where the sounds of blaring music could be felt and heard coming from Rodney's room. "Do you think Rodney is really innocent in all of this, Mom?" Taylor asked seriously. "I mean, he's fooled you before with the Mr. Nice Guy routine. This time it sounds like there could be some pretty rough consequences."

Susan sighed wearily. "I have to believe him, Taylor. I mean, the tether doesn't lie, so I've known where he's been every day. His drops have been clean, and he did agree to file for the protection orders. I really think Rodney's making changes. I just wish he hadn't gotten so angry today at the police station."

Taylor stood and stretched her arms above her head. "Listen, I'm going to go and catch up with my baby brother. Why don't you go take a little nap, and I'll wake you in a bit? I'm taking you both to dinner tonight, my treat, to celebrate my little visit," Taylor said, shaking her head as Susan began to protest.

"Mom, please just do what I'm asking you for once. I have a great job, I live in a beautiful condominium, and I make the most of my life. Let me take care of you for one night. After all, I'm not a baby," Taylor added, laughing. It had been her standard ending for all childhood arguments. Taylor had always wanted to press her independence. It was probably because of the havoc in their lives as her mom tried to maintain some semblance of normality while living with an abnormally controlling man.

"Fine, but you asked for it. I'm going to order something terribly expensive and not even try to pay the check when it arrives." Susan laughed, hugging Taylor as she moved around to check the alarm before they began to walk upstairs.

"I suggest an appetizer or two as well," Taylor taunted in fun, trying to ease the stress that had appeared on her mom's face as she watched the alarm lights.

"Keep it up little miss, and I might just order dessert too!" Taylor hugged her mom, holding her hard.

"It's good to be home with you, Mom," she said. "I've missed you so much."

"You are always welcome here, sweetheart," Susan said before going into her room to enjoy a sinful nap.

Taylor smiled as her mom shut the door and then turned to Rodney's door. "Maybe by you," she whispered, "but this one I'm still not so sure about."

Taylor took a deep breath and knocked on her brother's door. She was hoping there could be a civilized, intelligent conversation instead of the old routine of fighting and misunderstanding. She had come here for a reason, and she didn't want it to ruin her visit.

27

Rodney heard the knock and knew without looking that it was Taylor. *Could this day get any worse?* he wondered to himself. First there had been the mess with Melinda, then the visit to the police station, and now his sister's return.

Plus, he and his mom had just gotten into a cool space, and then Taylor arrives, screwing it all up with her perfectness. What a disaster today had turned into, and it wasn't even dinnertime yet. Rodney was in no mood to deal with Taylor, so he chose to ignore her instead. After a few minutes, he heard her walk away from his door, and he grinned at his cleverness in getting rid of her.

She probably planned on swooping down on him with some sort of lecture or pep talk, and Rodney wasn't interested in either. As soon as he heard the shower running in the bathroom next to his room, Rodney got up and checked the hallway to be sure Taylor wasn't spying. Since the coast was clear, he moved to his dresser and took out the cell phone that was hidden underneath a stash of old comic books. His mom had taken his phone away months ago, but she didn't know that he'd gotten another pay-as-you-go phone. His mom was on top of things, but Rodney had some tricks.

The number he hit was answered quickly. Melinda's stoned voice came through the phone line, and Rodney was filled with rage fueled by the day's events. "Mel, it's Rodney," he snarled.

"Well, if it isn't our own little prodigal son. Trying to return to the nest? Isn't that just too sweet, guys?" he heard her drawl to whoever was around her. "Nice try, Rod, but that just ain't gonna fly here. You are so out, as you must know after I had that little chat with your mommy," Melinda chuckled.

"Actually, I'm calling to give you notice, Mel," Rodney threatened in a voice that he reserved to frighten. "Come near my mom again, and I will take you out. Do you hear me? You know I never snitched on any of you, not even after Al left me to hang," he said. He was sure he had Melinda's attention now, as her comments, snide and otherwise, had stopped.

"You think we're afraid of you?" Melinda's drugged state was adding more bravado to her voice. "Bring it, you little bitch," she laughed into the phone. "We'll see how tough you are without us at your back," she added.

"Have you already forgotten who you're talking to Melinda?" Rodney's voice was dangerously low now. "Take a second and think about it. You know what I'm capable of Mel, so you and the crew are going to back off…immediately."

There was a profound silence on the other end of the line. Rodney knew Melinda was recalling things they had done in the past, and even high, she would recognize his words as the threat he had intended. Rodney might be on the right track, but Melinda wasn't going to threaten his mother without consequences.

"Yes, that's right, Mel. Think about what I said. I'm hanging up now, so you can go back to toasting your brains. Just remember, you stay away from me and mine. I haven't changed *that* much," he closed, clicking the phone shut.

Tucking the phone back in its hiding spot, Rodney went back to lie on his bed. He picked up the science fiction title he had been reading, and with a smile of satisfaction at a job well done, disappeared back into the story.

28

Susan awoke with a start, feeling disoriented and unsure of what time or day it was for a moment. Glancing at her bedside clock, she was shocked to realize she had slept for nearly two hours. She jumped up quickly, grabbing her bath towel, and went out into the hallway. She was surprised that Taylor hadn't woken her up earlier. The nap had truly been delicious, and Susan felt more like her old self.

Moving down the hall, Susan tapped on Taylor's door, entering when she heard Taylor's voice. Her daughter was sitting cross-legged on her childhood bed, and Susan was awash with flashbacks of Taylor as a teen.

"Hi there, Mom. Good nap?" Taylor asked, pushing her reading glasses up over her forehead. The laptop in front of Taylor was plugged in and humming with activity, and Susan couldn't help but smile at the contrast between the memories and the real Taylor.

"I was shocked I slept so long, but aside from feeling a bit decadent, I feel much better," Susan answered, gazing around the room. "Does it feel odd to be here?" she asked Taylor.

"Actually, it feels really good to be back, Mom. I'm sorry I stayed away for so long between visits. It's just..." Taylor's voice trailed away with a sigh.

"It's just that you needed to be sure you had forgiven me, for causing you such misery when you were younger. I know, baby," Susan said with a sad smile.

Taylor kept her head down for a moment, composing herself before she looked back at her mom. "It was not your fault about Joe, Mom. He was evil and you did get us out," Taylor added.

"Thank you for the olive branch; but it was my fault that we stayed for so long. And if we're going to be honest here, you saved me," Susan said as she moved to sit next to her oldest child.

Taylor leaned her body against Susan's, allowing Susan to stroke her hair and face gently as if she were six years old once again. The two of them had been through hell and back, and Susan knew it had taken great strength. Despite many years of counseling and the books she'd read, Susan had always cursed the amount of time it had taken her to finally leave Joe for good. She had read the statistics and knew that even though she had stayed much too long, she was still in the minority of abused women who survived. It was some comfort on the nights that Susan relived the horror of her abuse.

None of it mattered in the end, she finally realized, because she and her children were the true winners. She, Rodney, and Taylor were here now, in a wonderful home, safe and healthy. She knew that Joe had become another wheel in the justice system, and that one day he would likely die as a result of his violent behavior.

Susan pulled away from Taylor and looked down into the face that was so much like her own. "Do you know how amazing I think you are, my beautiful girl?" she said to Taylor. "Do not ever forget the power and strength that you possess inside yourself, Taylor. You are strong enough not to just survive. You are strong enough to live every day to its fullest. Trust me, honey, in order to really beat the past, we have to open our hearts up and love and trust people around us again."

Taylor hugged her arms around her mother a bit tighter and choked out a small laugh. "Wow, this Phillip must have really rocked your world, Mom," she said, not letting go of Susan as she tried to pull away in protest.

"Taylor Jasmeen Birge, you had better remember who you're talking to here," Susan laughed. "Now, let me go so I can go take a shower and get ready for the very expensive dinner I will be enjoying this evening. Did you tell Rodney?" Susan asked, "Or should I do that now?"

"He wouldn't let me into his room earlier, so I just left him alone. You should tell him," Taylor said, and as her stomach let out a growl added, "Tell him we're leaving in an hour!" Susan laughed and walked to Rodney's door to relay the message.

Knocking first, she went into Rodney's room to find her son engrossed in a novel. It was good to have both of her children around, and memories were rolling over her and filling her head with images of her sweet little babies. "We're leaving in an hour for dinner, Rodney," she said with a tap on his head when he didn't immediately look up from his absorption.

With a start, Rodney finally saw Susan, but she could tell he hadn't heard a word she'd said. She repeated the information, also letting him know they were going out, compliments of Taylor. "Finally," Rodney smiled, "the perfect way for retaliation. I am going to order the most expensive thing I can." He laughed both at the idea and the shocked expression on Susan's face.

"You will behave yourself, or you will suffer the wrath of Mom," she laughed, trying to make herself appear fierce and dangerous. She left her son to his novel and went to get ready. The day was going to be ending much better than it had started, and she was looking forward to it.

29

A couple of hours later, Susan sat in the same dining room she had with Phillip on their wonderful afternoon of revelations. She had ordered something new, an asparagus risotto, and was trying to get the recipe out of the maître d' so she could attempt it at home. Rodney had gone with a steak, as he usually did when they splurged and went out. Taylor had ordered a simple, yet delicious seafood pasta dish, and all three of them were enjoying the ambiance of the restaurant.

The dessert cart was making its way toward them, and Susan groaned in both protest and anticipation. Rodney was rubbing his hands together, leaning forward in pure glee. Taylor was actually laughing at her brother, and Susan couldn't remember a time when she'd been happier. She was suddenly positive that everything was going to work out. Phillip would handle the Melinda situation. Rodney would continue on his new path. Taylor would visit more often. She would open her heart to love. A smile of pure bliss was pasted on her face, and she was overwhelmed with good thoughts.

Rodney stood up as he finished his dessert. "I'm going to the little boy's room, and then head out to the deck to check out the view. If that's okay with you, Mom?" he added. Susan nodded her consent, thrilled with the change in Rodney's attitude and behavior.

As she watched her brother leave, Taylor turned to Susan with a nervous expression. "Rodney really seems like he's trying, Mom," Taylor said. "I didn't want to share this until I was sure you were in an okay place, but...I'm sorry, but I need to show you this," Taylor said, sliding a newspaper article over on the table. "I didn't know if you would want Rodney to see it, but I didn't want to tell you on the phone," she admitted.

Susan felt as if everything were moving in slow motion. A black-and-white photo of her ex-husband peered up at her from the table, his name clear underneath what must have been an earlier mug shot. The article was about a recent burglary gone wrong in a small New Jersey town. It stated that the culprit, one Joseph Birge, had been shot and killed in his attempt to escape. It went on to list Joe's many previous crimes without mention of any surviving family. Susan was grateful for that omission.

Susan wasn't sure she was still breathing. Aside from an occasional nightmare, she hadn't seen Joe's face in years. This photo held the same expression she remembered. Joe had passed down that expression to his son. She'd seen it on Rodney's face every time he tried to pass off his behavior as someone else's responsibility.

She allowed herself to remember how different Joe was when they first met. Susan had been left alone after her grandma died. She learned later that men like Joe found this trait irresistible. He wrapped his spell of entrapment around her through kind words, big promises, and a semblance of love. Once he married her, the face she saw in this photo began to appear.

That's what made it so hard to leave in the beginning. The first time he hurt her, Susan was in complete shock. Joe begged forgiveness, swearing it had all been his fault, a total mistake, and that he would never hurt her again. Susan still remembered the sting of his backhanded slap against her face. She remembered the grief. She remembered how desperately she wanted to believe his apology. Most of all, Susan remembered how it felt when that first small sliver of herself broke away.

Tears were spilling from her eyes as she looked up at Taylor. Clearing her choked throat, she asked, "Why do you have this?"

"I've been keeping track of him for years, Mom," Taylor admitted. "I used to have nightmares that I woke up and Joe was standing above me. I realized that for my own peace of mind I needed to know what he was up to. It let me sleep soundly. I knew you would be upset, so I never told you. I was always afraid that you'd find out, so I tried to stay away as much as I could," she said. "I never stayed away because I blamed you, Mom. It wasn't our fault. It was always his," she said, jabbing her finger into the photo that sat between them on the table.

The moment was broken by Rodney's exuberant voice. "You guys should come out here and see the view! It's so amazing!" Susan fisted the paper in her hand, pulling it into her lap before Rodney could see. When he saw Susan's face, though, Rodney could tell that something had been going on between her and Taylor.

"What's wrong? Taylor, what did you do?" Rodney asked, concerned and angry that he had been left out of something important.

"It's nothing, honey," Susan said. "Taylor and I were just catching up, and you know me, I got all emotional." Susan saw Rodney watching both of them, and though he didn't seem convinced, he let the matter go.

The waiter showed up then with the check, placing it on the edge next to Taylor. Susan reflexively reached for it, forgetting the paper clipping in her hand. As Taylor reached for the check to stop her mother, Rodney reached out and snapped the paper from Susan's hand.

"Rodney, NO!" Susan said louder than she had intended. Rodney quickly unfolded the paper, and turned to stone. He held the words close to his face, reading them carefully. His forehead scrunched in confusion, as Susan tried to explain. "Rodney, please, listen to me," she tried.

Directing his glare at Taylor, Rodney asked between clenched teeth, "You've known where he was the whole time, haven't you? Didn't you think I should know where Dad was, Taylor? Isn't it bad enough that you had all the time with him that I never did? Did you have to steal him from me now too?" Rodney was breathing hard, and Susan was worried that he was going to lose it completely.

"Rodney, listen to me," Susan said, standing and trying to get Rodney to sit back down at the table. "We will talk about this more at home, but right now you need to calm down. Please!"

Rodney finally looked at Susan, and there was such hatred behind his eyes that she was caught off balance. "All these years that I could have had with my dad, and you just left him alone. I always knew that you loved Taylor more than me, Mom, but to keep me from my own dad? How could you?"

Susan was shocked. It had been so long since Rodney had asked her about Joe. Obviously he'd been harboring this rage a while. "Rodney, did you read the whole article?" Susan asked him softly. Apparently Rodney wasn't going to let this conversation go until they got home. She needed to do her best to deflate the worst of it now.

"Yeah, it says he died. My dad died alone, probably not even knowing I was alive," Rodney said.

Taylor burst in at this point. "It also says that dear old Dad was a criminal. He was holding someone hostage, at gunpoint, Rodney. He was shot down trying to rob a bank. If you read all of it, and I know you can read little brother, what it really says is that we are finally free worrying about Joe Birge showing up!"

"You shut up!" Rodney yelled at Taylor.

"You just didn't want him anymore," Rodney now directed his anger at Susan, "so you threw him out. What's the matter, Mom, did you find some great cop and get tired of my dad?"

Susan felt the carefully stacked pieces of her life tumbling down around her. This day was destined to be her worst. She watched her son's face meld into the angry memory of Joe's and shook herself to clear her head.

Taylor couldn't stay quiet any longer though. "Really, Rodney? You want to believe so badly in that little fantasy of yours?" she seethed at him. "Well, let me tell you what your beloved father did," she said to him.

Before she could explain, Rodney stood from the table, which had so recently held one of Susan's best memories. "I don't need to listen to you, Taylor. I don't have to listen to either of your lies anymore," he said, and shoving the article into his shirt pocket Rodney moved quickly out of the restaurant.

Susan stood, trying to stop him. "You go and get him, Mom," Taylor said. "I'll pay the bill and meet you at the car. It'll be all right. It was time for him to grow up and face the truth anyway," she added. "Go on," Taylor said, moving to the waiter with her purse in hand.

Susan rushed out of the restaurant toward Taylor's car. Rodney was nowhere to be found, and Susan felt the familiar panic overwhelm her. "Rodney!" she began to call. "Rodney, please answer me!" she called again.

Her cell phone beeped in the darkness, and Susan saw that it was Phillip. She felt a surge of relief. "Oh, thank God, Phillip," she said into the phone.

"Susan, I was just calling to see how your reunion dinner went." Susan quickly filled Phillip in on what had happened that evening, sure that he could handle the truth of her past. She was more relieved than ever that she'd already told him so much.

"Meet me at your house, Susan. I have a feeling that's where he'll be heading. Try not to alert too many people, and we'll see if we can get Rodney back under control without too much damage."

"Thank you so much," Susan said as Taylor came up beside her in the parking lot.

Taylor realized that Rodney wasn't in the car and looked at Susan with concern. "Mom, I'm sorry. I should have waited until we were home, but I couldn't keep it inside any more," she sobbed.

"Taylor, this isn't your fault. Your brother needed to know. Maybe I should have told him more before tonight, but he quit asking. I thought he'd let go of the idea of finding your father," Susan said as she got into the car. "Right now, we need to get home. Phillip is meeting us there and we'll figure out what to do next. If Rodney really has taken off, though, the authorities will have to get involved since it breaks his probation. Plus, I'm worried about the crew," she said. It was a tense, silent drive home filled with dread as to what could possibly happen next.

30

Taylor drove home as quickly as she could, but Phillip was already waiting for them when they got there. Susan walked into his arms, and a sob broke from her in relief. It felt good having a shoulder to lean against. It was obvious that Rodney hadn't come back to the house as they approached the dark building.

Susan opened the door and pushed in the alarm code, flipping on the light switch. The house looked just like it had when they left, and Susan was shocked. It seemed like there should be more disruption to match what was happening inside of her. This could be the very thing to send Rodney back to his former life, and she was dying a little bit with every second that passed.

The phone rang loudly in the quiet, and Susan leaped toward the sound. "Hello, Rodney?" she said without waiting to see who it was. Susan's shoulders dropped a bit when it wasn't her son, but as she heard Veronica's voice a surge of relief rushed through her.

"He's there with you?" Susan said as she sank to her knees on the kitchen floor. She looked up at Taylor. "Yes, we'll be here. Thank you, Veronica," Susan said before hanging up and beginning to cry.

"That was Veronica, Rodney's tutor. He went to her house. I guess he ran all the way there. She's convinced him he needs to come home," Susan said as Phillip helped her to her feet.

Taylor started to make a pot of coffee. "Looks like we might need this, huh?"

Susan smiled and nodded, looking at Phillip. "Thank goodness," Susan said to him. "Maybe Rodney has changed. In the past he would have just gone, or met the crew and lost himself for the night in drugs and alcohol."

"You believed in him, Susan. More than you should have some would say," he said looking over at Taylor, who nodded in agreement.

"So, does this have to go on some kind of report then, Officer Reynolds?" Taylor asked. "Is this going to ruin my little brother's chance of getting straightened up?"

"For now, Rodney's making good decisions. I can only imagine the shock he had when he saw the article with his father's picture on it. From what your mom has told me, Joe Birge was a true criminal, but it would still be a blow to learn your father has died. Plus, there goes the little boy's dream of his mom and dad getting back together."

Susan started to protest.

"I know that was never going to happen, Susan. You know that was never going to happen, but Rodney? I've seen it over and over again. No matter how old the kids are they cling to that dream until they're grown up enough to see that being together isn't best."

"So?" Taylor asked again.

Phillip was prevented from answering as the crunch of tires on gravel, followed shortly by the shutting of two car doors, alerted the kitchen inhabitants that Rodney and Veronica had made it to the house. Susan sat completely still at the table, while Taylor and Phillip stood nearby. Rodney came in first, looking abashed. He stood in the doorway, not saying a word, watching Susan.

"I'm so sorry," Susan whispered to Rodney. It was as if they were alone in the room. "I should have told you about your dad a long time ago," she said, sobbing with the last word.

Rodney was shoved gently from behind, and then answered Susan. "I'm sorry too, Mom," he admitted. "I know you were trying to protect me," he added, "but I was pretty pissed. I had to run or explode. I knew Veronica would listen. I told her everything."

With this, he pulled the arm of the girl behind him so she stood beside him in the kitchen.

Susan looked up at the young woman and smiled at the beauty before her, knowing instantly why Rodney had taken to her so strongly.

"It's nice to meet you, Ms. Birge," Veronica said.

"Nice to meet you too, Veronica," Susan said.

"Well," Veronica said. "I should be going, so all of you can talk this out."

Rodney began to protest, but Veronica stopped him. "Listen, you need to do this. Call me tomorrow." Susan was surprised to watch her son give in and agree, walking Veronica to the door, giving her a hug and a quick kiss as she left.

When Rodney turned back into the room, all sets of eyes were on him. "What?" he asked. "If you can have a secret boyfriend, then I can have a secret girlfriend," he said.

There was a moment of shocked silence, and then Taylor moved to stand next to her brother. "Yeah, Mom. Fair is fair," she said. It was the much needed mood breaker in the room, causing everyone to laugh.

Phillip moved to shake Rodney's hand. "I'm glad you decided to come back, Rodney. I haven't logged the tether alert yet, but know that it will be noted as a malfunction of equipment," he added. Tapping Rodney's forehead gently, he added, "Every now and then we all have equipment malfunctions, kid."

"Thanks, Officer Reynolds," Rodney answered. "Do you think I'll still be able to have the tether removed this week like we had talked about?"

Phillip smiled and nodded. "It's probably time, Rodney. At this point, you'll either do right or not; and based on what I've seen, my money is on you doing the right thing from here on out."

Rodney seemed to grow taller before Susan's eyes. It had been too long since Rodney had a positive male role model. Maybe everything was going to be all right after all.

Taylor let out a huge yawn, and Phillip decided it was time for him to go. "Get some sleep, everyone," he said his eyes never leaving Susan's face as she smiled.

"I'll call you tomorrow," Susan said to him. "Thank you for everything," she said as he left.

"Don't forget to reset the alarm!" Phillip yelled from the front walkway. Susan laughed, but moved right over and did just that. Until Melinda's threats were resolved, Susan wasn't taking any extra chances, especially now that Rodney was home.

Hugging her children at each of their doorways, she smiled as they awkwardly hugged each other good night too. Taylor's door clicked shut as Susan stood next to Rodney.

Turning to Rodney, Susan said, "You know we're not done talking about all of this. Right?"

"I know. I think we both need that," Rodney answered. "I love you, Mom," he added before closing his door.

Susan rested the palm of her hand lightly on the closed door. There were still many ups and downs ahead of them on this roller coaster ride, but at least Rodney seemed on board with it now. Making her way into bed and snuggling under a heavy down comforter, Susan was sure she'd barely hit the pillow before exhaustion claimed her.

31

The silence woke Rodney. His digital clock read three in the morning. He hadn't heard anything, but he felt something ominous in the quiet inside the house. He leaned up on his elbow and that was when he heard the squeak on the stairs. It stopped as suddenly as it had sounded, but Rodney's body went on full alert.

Someone was in the house, and he was sure it was Melinda.

He knew the crew was adept at getting around alarm systems. It was one reason he'd made the call to her. He'd hoped to deter them, but apparently it hadn't worked. Rodney reached into his drawer and pulled out the phone he had hidden there. It was only used now for emergencies, and Rodney was pretty sure this counted.

Whispering into the phone, he gave the 9-1-1 operator his address, telling her someone had broken into his house. He did not disconnect, but left the open phone on his nightstand as he slowly got out of bed.

Rodney picked up the baseball bat from behind his door. He had moved it there after the incident with his mom. She'd nearly taken his head off, and he felt a little safer with the bat in his room. After the years she and Taylor had protected him, Rodney knew it was his turn to protect them from his mess.

Melinda knew which room was his, having snuck in numerous times. Rodney could only hope that the crew would be concentrating on coming after him and not anyone else in the house. As far as he knew, they didn't know about Taylor being here, but he couldn't be sure. The group was fairly good at casing a joint before they made entry, so Rodney had to assume they had seen what had happened earlier this evening.

Silently, Rodney moved to crouch in front of his dresser, pulling the bat into swinging position. He saw the doorknob turn slowly, and readied himself for action. From where he crouched, the person behind the door wouldn't be able to see him, and Rodney was hoping he could get a swing at their knees and take them out before they got in a shot of their own.

Without a sound, the legs moved into view, and Rodney allowed his eyes to scan upward. His old friend, Alan, was creeping into his room, a steel bar in his hands. So, Rodney thought, the crew had sent in the second string, hoping to beat Rodney in his sleep, leaving him to be found by his mom in the morning. It was a pretty decent plan, Rodney had to admit, if you were a sadistic kind of person.

Rodney watched Alan take another silent step, raising the steel bar over his head. Alan started to swing downward toward the lump of blankets that could have been Rodney's head on the pillow. Rodney put all of his power into swinging the baseball bat into Alan's shins.

Alan's scream was so loud it should have woken the dead. Rodney knew that if Melinda and the rest of the crew were nearby they would most likely abandon the plan and run. Alan was screaming, trying to wrap his arms around his bashed legs. He looked up in surprise at Rodney, who stood over him now, ready to swing again. The old Rodney would have continued swinging, but now he simply leaned over and grabbed the steel pipe out of Alan's reach.

Rodney could faintly hear the 9-1-1 operator, asking what was going on, telling the empty receiver that help was on the way.

Rodney turned as both Taylor and his mom came running into the doorway, aghast at the scene before them. Rodney started to explain, but Alan's screams were too loud.

"Dude, shut up!" Rodney leaned down and screamed into Alan's face. Instantly, Alan was silent, only an occasional moan escaping his mouth.

Rodney turned back to his mom and started to move toward her; and that was when he heard the click of a gun's hammer from the hall. Everyone froze, and Rodney saw his mother's eyes lock on his own.

"Well, looks like this little party isn't going as planned folks," said Melinda's slurred voice. He saw his mom jerk as Melinda jammed the end of the gun into her back.

"Let's move into the room please, Mommy," Melinda said, shoving the gun harder into Susan's back. "You too, Princess," Melinda added with a nod at Taylor. His mom and sister moved to stand by Rodney.

Rodney's room was suddenly lit by the full moon's light as Melinda yanked open the shade. She sneered down at Alan. "You couldn't even do this right? I should just shoot you right here," Melinda said, pointing the gun for a moment at Alan and laughing.

Rodney knew this couldn't end well. Melinda's glazed eyes were testimony to her drugged state, and Rodney remembered well the feeling of invincibility. She wouldn't stop until she'd completed her crazy plan, and Rodney was desperately trying to think of a way to get his family out of the room.

"Melinda," Rodney said softly to the girl he used to consider one of his best friends. "It's me you want. Here I am." Rodney moved slightly closer to his mom and Taylor, trying to put himself between them and Melinda. Alan's moaning body had become a rather awkward midline in the room, with Melinda on one side and Rodney and his family on the other. Unfortunately, Melinda was closer to the door. However, standing as they were, Rodney also knew that Melinda couldn't see the opened phone. If he wasn't able to get Taylor and his mom out of the room, Rodney was hoping to at least block them from her rage.

Melinda laughed harshly, wiping her free hand over her nose. "Oh, what's this Rodney, are you all protective now? I remember all the shit you told me about these two bitches."

Rodney watched his mom, and he pleaded with his eyes for her to understand. His mom tried to smile at him. She meant so much to him, Rodney realized. No matter what, he hoped she knew he was a different person now.

Rodney's resolve to get them out of this mess strengthened. He knew that at any minute the sound of police sirens would alert Melinda. In her current state he wasn't sure how she'd react. He knew the only way to protect his family was to play into Melinda's ego.

"Yeah, you're right, Melinda," Rodney said to her with his old swagger and bravado. "It's too bad you didn't listen to me earlier. You had to go and screw it all up for me."

Melinda looked as confused as Taylor and his mom, but Rodney could only hope his mom would figure out the ruse he was using to save them.

"What are you talking about now, Rod?" Melinda asked him, doubt clearly in her voice.

"I mean, if you hadn't sent this moron in here tonight, by tomorrow I could have been free and clear of this hell hole, with a big old bankroll to boot!" Rodney said, moving away from his family and closer to Melinda.

Melinda had dropped the gun a bit, but as Rodney moved, she yanked it up again. Rodney forced his body to stay calm, shaking his head at Melinda. "Where's the rest of the crew, Melinda?" he asked her, as if he were back in charge again.

"That bunch of cowards?" Melinda sneered. "They all backed out, too chicken-shit to follow through with my plan. Ever since you left they haven't been listening like they're supposed to. Me and Alan had to pull this one off ourselves." Melinda kicked Alan in the ribs, "Lot of help he turned out to be though."

"Well, looks like it's just you and me, Mel," Rodney said, stepping over Alan's prone form to stand next to her. "Look, I know where my mom keeps the money, so let's go get it. We can get out of here before they can even call the cops," Rodney said as sincerely as possible. Without looking back at his sister and mother, Rodney began to lead Melinda out of the bedroom.

"What about me?" Alan finally yelled from the floor.

"Screw you!" Rodney declared. "You remember when you left me hanging for the cops? Looks like you owe me one, pal." Melinda laughed at Rodney's words, walking unsteadily with him into the hallway.

"So, where's the cash?" Melinda asked Rodney.

As soon as Melinda walked into the hallway, Rodney reached around and locked his door, pulling it shut behind them. He also threw the deadbolt on the outside, a safety precaution his mom had installed during his troubled days. He knew Melinda wouldn't be able to get to them now, and that was Rodney's main concern.

As Melinda turned toward him, Rodney made a lunge for the gun in her hand. The drugs made her react more slowly, but also gave her unusual strength. Melinda's moment of surprise was quickly replaced by rage as she realized she'd been duped by Rodney's deception. She shoved her body hard against Rodney, slamming him back into the doorway he had just closed.

"I'm going to kill you!" she screamed.

Rodney could hear his mom yelling at him from his locked room. He tried to block it out as he concentrated on fighting off Melinda. If he could only keep her contained until the police arrived, Taylor and his mom would be okay. He shoved back against Melinda, twisting her away from the door.

"I'm going to kill you, and then I'm going back in there and finish off those two," Melinda yelled, trying to twist her wrists and the gun free of Rodney's grasp.

"You are never going to hurt them," Rodney screamed back, hurtling them farther down the hallway. He realized that they were moving toward the staircase, and Rodney knew if he could get to the first floor his family should be safe. Melinda could only concentrate on the gun in her hands, and Rodney kept his grip firmly on the revolver. He knew Melinda would shoot him without hesitating if she could wrestle the gun away.

Rodney pushed even harder, using his height advantage against Melinda's smaller, petite form. He had moved them just a few inches from the stairs when he heard the sirens wailing toward his house. Time seemed to freeze as Rodney saw Melinda's recognition as well.

Suddenly, Rodney could hear clearly the sounds in the house. The sirens racing. His mom yelling his name. The pounding on the door, unable to get to him because of the lock he had set. Melinda's snarling face was spitting mad, and Rodney could feel the gun slipping out of his grasp as her drug-induced strength began to overwhelm his own.

With a last desperate push, Rodney felt their bodies fall toward the staircase. Melinda's face changed as she realized what was happening, and Rodney released the gun and wrapped his arms around her to prevent her escape. Their bodies tumbled down the stairs, and Rodney held on for dear life. He heard the explosion of the gun, but held on despite the pain as his body smashed against the hard wooden stairs, rolling together with Melinda's.

Before Rodney hit the bottom, he heard the front door being smashed in and the sounds of police entering the room. He knew then that his mom would be okay and finally gave in to oblivion. He could hear his mom next to him then, and felt her gentle touch against his forehead.

32

Susan stood very still, looking at the flowers she had arranged. There were a large mixture of sizes and textures and colors, and yet it all worked so well together. She couldn't help but remember another arrangement she'd made, one that had ended up on Phillip's table to be unappreciated by Tubs.

In the very center of this arrangement there was a cluster of ordinary white roses. White roses stood for strength, and were not usually the first choice of most people for a grouping. Susan knew how special they were, though, and how misunderstood they sometimes were as well. She had chosen them especially for the arrangement she had put together for today. Her gaze was intent on the roses, as she gently stroked the petals.

Phillip whispered her name from where he stood beside her, and Susan was brought back to her surroundings. She looked to her left and saw her daughter, Taylor, standing there as well. Taylor was trying to smile, but tears escaped her beautiful eyes. Susan looked back to Phillip, and he took her elbow and led her forward on shaky legs.

Susan stood beside the man she had begun to love and breathed in the aroma of the flowers she held. Tears ran down her face, and she looked up at Phillip for confirmation. Phillip ran a soft touch down Susan's face and nodded.

With a deep breath, Susan finally looked at the dark ebony of the casket in front of her. She had always known that her son was destined for something great, and he had proven that in the end. Rodney had sacrificed his life to save the lives of his family. The fall down the stairs had nearly killed Melinda, but it was the shot from the gun that had killed her son.

Susan stared at the newly upturned ground, remembering how she had rushed from the room as the lock finally gave. She had raced down the stairs, to find her son's bleeding body in her kitchen.

She thought he was dead, but Rodney smiled as she stroked her fingers across his forehead, whispering that it would all be fine. Susan knew that he could hear her and kept telling Rodney things she loved about him. She reminded him of the fancy napkins and the girlfriend who was waiting for him to call her. She stroked her baby's face and cried, fighting off the panic as she heard the ambulance in the night approaching her home.

Taylor stood behind her, sobbing silently as they watched the life leave Rodney. Susan held Rodney to her tightly, telling him how much she loved him, and that he would be happy now, able to read all day, and sleep in as long as he wanted. Knowing the moment he took his final breath, the screams raged from Susan one after another. She howled with loss and pain. Rocking her baby's lifeless body in her arms, she was unaware of anything else as she held on and screamed.

Phillip arrived and helped the paramedics pull her away from Rodney. There were questions to be answered and Susan watched it all as if from a distance. She watched as Alan's battered body was brought down and taken to the hospital along with Melinda's unconscious form. She watched as strangers laid her son's body on the gurney and took him from his home.

And now here she stood, surrounded by Miss Bell, Rodney's favorite teacher, and other teachers from Oxford High School. The tough looking Mr. Kruse held the trophy that Rodney had earned playing basketball. When he'd approached Susan that morning and shared the story, it was a breath of joy and relief for her. He'd promised to hold onto the gaudy prize until Susan was ready to take it home.

Mr. Rodriguez and Mr. Oakes were nearby, along with a group of young men and a little girl who clutched a teddy bear and had not stopped crying during the graveside ceremony. Veronica stood quietly on the other side of Taylor, and the two seemed to find support in each other.

The preacher had stopped talking, and Susan stroked the white roses one last time. Reaching back for Phillip's support, she felt his fingers squeeze her right hand. His grip gave Susan strength. She leaned forward and placed the flowers for Rodney on top of the coffin. Her heart was shattering in ways she'd never imagined, as she said good-bye to the son who would never smile at her again.

The flowers lay stark against the darkness of the coffin, as the sun suddenly broke free of the clouds, shining down on them in their grief. Susan took a small step back to stand beside Phillip, and Taylor took a step forward to lean against her shoulder. Rodney had brought them all together. She knew she had to live a stronger life, despite wanting to simply give in to her heartache, because of what Rodney had given her in his final moments.

Susan looked up at the blue sky. "Now you've both saved my life, Rodney," she whispered.

As the guests began to depart, leaving her to stand with Phillip and Taylor, she looked down at Rodney's flowers. Pulling her shoulders back, Susan wiped her eyes and sniffed back her sob. Phillip pulled a handkerchief from his pocket, handing it to Susan. They began to walk to the car that waited to take her to his home, where guests were gathering to share memories of Rodney's life.

As Susan looked at the linen handkerchief, she heard Rodney's little-boy voice say in wonder, "Look, Mommy, it's a fancy napkin." Susan wrapped an arm around Taylor and Phillip, smiling through fresh tears. As the car pulled away from the roadside, Susan looked back. The last thing she saw were the flowers, lit by the sun, a testament of her love for Rodney.

THE END

ABOUT THE AUTHOR

Kristine E. Brickey lives in a small Michigan town with her husband, two dogs, donkeys, and her horse, Snickers. The mother of two, she has also spent twenty-six years teaching children in the public school system—nine years in elementary and seventeen in middle school, with a focus on language arts.

Brickey holds a master's degree in reading and is particularly interested in working with boys and literacy issues. She is always looking for ways to encourage young writers as well as young readers and started a middle school writing club to promote opportunities for her students.

Inspired by a conversation with her son, Brickey wrote the candid and poignant YA novel *Flowers for Rodney* to inspire teens and start an honest conversation that parents can engage in with their children.

21553892R00099

Made in the USA
Middletown, DE
03 July 2015